The Magic
of the Wolves

A Collection of Children's Stories

Silver

FAYE STINE

Outskirts Press, Inc.
Denver, Colorado

The Magic of the Wolves
A Collection of Children's Stories
All Rights Reserved.
Copyright © 2011 Faye Stine
v1.0

Outskirts Press, Inc.
http://www.outskirtspress.com

ISBN: 978-1-4327-7864-4

Library of Congress Control Number: 2011911837

Outskirts Press and the "OP" logo are trademarks belonging to Outskirts Press, Inc.

PRINTED IN THE UNITED STATES OF AMERICA

Contents

Tina of the North Country

K eith lived with his parents, Frank and Ellen Moore, on their acres of apple orchards in northern Washington. Their house, or hacienda as the native Indians called it, was over 100 years old, and some remembered the stories of the settling of the white man in their country. Many a brave warrior was remembered. The house was surely a fortress of gold-colored stucco and could be seen throughout the valley surrounding the house. The Moores' apple orchards stretched for many miles, and the apples were known worldwide as Moores' golden delicious apples.

They were close enough to Alaska to see the aurora borealis every night in the skies over their ranch. It was a wondrous sight of blue and green lights and a majestic scene to all viewers. It was really a wonder of nature. Keith and his family spent many a night watching these lights and remarking on their beauty.

Keith's family were farmers, and the forest surrounding their ranch was plentiful with game, especially deer. The wolves guarded their territory in the forest but were tolerant of man, who they had bonded with years before.

There were many Indian legends about the wolves. It was said there was a supernatural alpha female, black with silver slashes and a silver ruff, called Tina—a legend in her own right. She was a dauntless leader of the pack and ruled with the alpha male Silver, whom no other wolf could equal.

It was also said that when man was in danger, the wolves would appear to help him. Many Indians believed the wolves had sacred powers and would appear in forms other than wolves. Many times the Indians consulted the god of the forest, Kahula, to ask the wolves for special favors.

Many nights Keith's parents discussed these stories about the wolves while Keith listened attentively before he went to bed. One night he had a dream that he saw Tina, the alpha leader of the pack, and he flew on her back to the stars and met other wolves there. They all played happily with him.

When he told his mother about this dream, she told him, "You just had a dream. Wolves don't fly. Now do your homework."

But Keith was not too sure and wanted to meet Tina, the wolf legend. He helped his mother with the chores in the morning and in the afternoon napped on the backyard patio after lunch with her. Sometimes as a special treat he rode in his father's truck while his father oversaw the harvesting of the apples. Keith, like all curious boys his age, always wanted to explore. Keith was a full six years of boundless energy, and he had always wanted to see Tina, the legendary wolf of the forest.

One day while his mother was sleeping, he set out to do just that. Unknown to Ellen, Keith slipped under the outer evergreens of the closed backyard's penetrable hedges that separated the yard from the nearby forest. He was off to find Tina, the legendary wolf of the forest and legend of the Indian's god of the forest, Kahula.

Keith walked along the road until he finally saw a path opened by the deer to the forest. He followed it until he came to a lovely meadow of grasses and wild flowers and some berry bushes. Hungrily he ate his fill.

No Tina yet, he thought. He then continued on walking in the bush.

Keith found himself by a river. His mother had warned him that bears were in the forest and never to go into the forest alone. But Keith the adventurer did not heed her warning.

He walked on by the river and turned the bend. There in front of him, down the lane, was a black bear and her two cubs.

Keith gasped. *Oh my gosh, what should I do?* he thought. He then let out a fearful cry. He really had never seen a bear before and was frightened. It was so big.

But the bear had seen Keith and was about to charge. Suddenly Keith heard the shrill howl of the wolf. It was Tina, who had been watching over this small person and knew Keith was in trouble.

As if in a dream, a stream of wolves appeared from the forest edge. Silver, the alpha male, led the pack in an attack group with Tina walking with him deliberately towards the bear. Silver signaled the pack to attack only on his command, for taking the bear down would incur injuries to the pack. The bear stood on her hind legs, growling and menacing and shaking her paws. Then with her two cubs in front of her, she retreated into the forest. Silver signaled two of the pack to follow the bear to be sure she had left their territory.

At the sight of the bears' disappearance, Tina howled her victory and soon all the others howled with her. It was a sound that echoed through the forest. It was the sound of victory.

Now was the time to celebrate their success. As quickly as the chasing of the bear had ended, the playing of the wolf cubs began. The cubs lay on their backs and the sibling brothers and sisters jumped over and above them. They ran in circles and played wolf tag. Finally, the cubs dropped from exhaustion. The older wolves watched attentively and never lowered their gaze. Tina and Silver were foremost in the frolic, enjoying every bit of it.

Keith was delighted at the games. He ran up and down the sides of the pack clapping his hands and chasing the cubs and petting them.

"Hello, Wolfie. Hello, Wolfie. It's Keith. I want to be your friend."

Indeed Keith was to all of the wolf pack cubs. They accepted him as one of their own, playing and scampering with him. Tina, the wise mother, watched over Keith as if he were one of her own cubs, never taking her eyes off them or him. At last Keith had found Tina, and what a friend she was to him.

The wolf cubs, tired of their play, went back to the den to rest and eat. The den was a moss-covered opening by a large cedar tree with a tunnel to a warm place for Tina's caring of her cubs. Keith followed the cubs and soon found himself in Tina's den and alone with Tina and her cubs. Oh happy day. It was getting dark out and he also decided to rest from his adventures with the bear and Tina's cubs. Soon he was in an exhausted sleep, and Tina's warm body was next to him, protecting him and sheltering him from the cold. Her cubs were at her side, snuggling warm next to her.

Keith woke up the next morning to find there was all activity going on around him. The cubs were hungrily suckling their breakfast, and there beside him was a layer of huckleberries Tina had left for him. Tina hadn't forgotten her newfound friend she rescued from the bear. Keith ate the berries hungrily.

While Keith was resting in the den, Silver, the white male, appeared. He was seeking his mate, Tina, and their cubs and was also noticing Keith, the boy child Tina had protected with their pack.

Immediately Keith spoke to him. "I am Keith. I want to be your friend."

The alpha male looked at Keith without a nod, as if he shouldn't be in his den. He acted as though Keith were an intruder. But Keith pursued the friendship. He patted Silver under his chin, and his cause was won. Their friendship was made. The patting sent signals through Silver's body and he then wagged his tale in friendship and trust.

Tina was watching all this and whirled to meet Silver. She went to him with such joy, a joy that she would rarely show anyone but Silver. Her mate had accepted her adopted cub Keith into their pack. Then Silver left as quickly as he had come. Peace came to the sleeping den once again. Tina continued to feed her pups, and Keith waited for the dawn to start for home.

Although he would miss Tina and her friends, he knew he must go home. He also knew this adventure of his had frightened his mother and that his father would be looking for him. Keith then pet Tina, who returned his friendship, and left to find his way back home.

Keith found the river close by to the den and followed along the banks where he had met the bear. Soon he rounded the bend by the river and found himself in the meadows and again hungrily ate the huckleberries there. Now he finally saw the path that had taken him to the meadows and he followed it to find its entrance. He soon heard his father's voice and knew he was now safe.

"Keith, Keith, where are you, son? It's Father. Answer me."

And Keith did just that. "Here I am, Father, on the path. Come find me!"

His father did just that. "Keith, where were you? Your mother is frantic. You must never do this again. Your uncle Jack and I were both out looking for you."

Jack then joined Keith and his father. He had also heard Keith on the path. "Keith, we were frantic. Why did you go into the forest alone?" he asked.

"I wanted to see the legend of the Indians, the wolf Tina," he told them.

"Did you?" they asked.

"Yes, I did. She is truly wonderful. She appeared out of the forest with her pack and saved me from a bear by the river. I owe her my life," he explained. "It was dark and she took me to her cave and I played with her cubs. It was warm in her cave, but it was dark outside and cold."

"We must go right home. You must promise your mother you will never do this again. Tina belongs in her home in the forest and you belong in your home with us."

"I will stay where I belong at home with my mother, I promise," Keith told his father and uncle. "But someday I will return to forest when I am a grown man, and I know she will be waiting for me again as she was then. I will be with Tina again."

Keith and his father proceeded down the path to the house and his mother, who was waiting for him. With frantic tears and outstretched arms she embraced Keith. "Where did you go?" she asked.

"I went to see Tina, the legendary wolf of the forest," he answered.

"Is she all the Indians say she is?" his mother asked.

"Yes, Mother, that and more. She saved my life when I was almost attacked by a bear. I owe her much thanks. She sheltered me in her den and I played with her cubs. The wolves all were friends to me. I love them."

"Keith, you must promise never to go alone again into the forest. There is much danger there." His mother spoke quietly but firmly.

"I promise, but I will return to see Tina when I am a man. I know she will be waiting for me."

"Yes, Keith, you may when you are a man," she agreed. Then Frank and Ellen and Jack sat and listened all afternoon to his adventure with Tina and the wolf pack. They were astounded at what he told them.

This story of Keith and the magic wolf, Tina, was not over. As Keith promised, he would return to Tina, and she would be waiting for him.

Keith never forgot Tina and the alpha wolf Silver during his adolescence. He spoke of his friendship with them many times to his parents. They agreed with him: Tina and Silver were truly his friends. They had saved him from a harrowing experience with the bear.

Keith's father was a successful planter and decided to expand his valuable land of apple orchards to include Bartlett pears. Frank Moore arranged to add 100 additional acres, and with Keith now an adolescent, they rode over the range, overseeing the harvesting of the apples and the growing of the new crop of pears. He and Keith many times felt the friendship of the wolves while riding. The wolves ran freely through the forest. Their silhouettes shadowed the moon. Many times their calls of friendship to each other were heard through the night as they had done many centuries before.

The Indians now owning small farms did not fear the wolves. They saw them as fearless and having great supernatural powers and wisdom. Many times they asked the spirits of the wolves for guidance, especially if a crop failed or cattle died or they were in danger of losing a child.

Such was the adolescence of Keith—overseeing their orchards with his father and waiting for his manhood to see Tina again. Keith knew Tina was protecting the territory that nature gave her, and she and Silver were waiting for him.

Keith went to a school in a nearby city and was an honor student, intending to go to agriculture college in the fall.

Keith's mother Ellen heard the wolves' calls at night and asked Keith, "Have you ever seen Tina, the wolf that saved you from the bear when you were so young?"

"No, Mother, but I have heard her calls and I know she is waiting for me. I will be with her again someday. She and I will be happy to see each other again. I will wait just a few more years, when I am older. Do I have your permission, Mother?"

"Of course you do. You are the man your father is. I will not worry," she answered.

"The Indians are right, Mother. The wolves are the true rulers of the forest. "I will see Tina someday and we will share our friendship as we did before."

"Yes, you will," his mother answered.

Night after night Keith and his family watched the splendor of the aurora borealis and spoke many times of his adventures with Tina— how she watched over him and how she and her pack saved him from the angry bear. When the Indians heard the story, they knew she was the spirit of the wolf, a mystical and powerful creature.

Many nights after dark from the house Keith heard Tina's friendly call urging him to come back to the forest, and he knew someday he would be with her again. Close to dawn on one such night, when he was resting after riding on the land with his father, he heard a soft whimper. He knew an animal outside his room was in trouble. When he went to the yard, there was Tina bent over a bloodied paw. She had come to Keith for help.

Whatever has happened to Tina? he thought. *Has she been attacked?*

"Tina, my friend, how did you get so hurt?" He spoke to her quietly in the darkness.

Although she could not speak to him, she rolled her piercing amber eyes and whimpered her answer. Keith guessed she had been attacked by a larger animal, probably a bear. Most likely the bear she had saved him from. Keith was strong for an adolescent. He picked Tina up and carried her to the kitchen and laid her on the table. His father, hearing the noises, entered the kitchen.

"Father, Father, Tina has been hurt. Her paw is bloodied and wounded to the bone. I think it's the same bear she fought off for me."

"You are probably right, Keith. Let me help you. I have a first aid kit. Lay Tina on the table and I will dress the wound," he said.

Frank Moore expertly cleaned the wound and applied an antiseptic bandage. Tina lay still, not moving. She trusted Keith and his father. After the wound was cleaned and bandaged, Keith sat with Tina and cradled her head in his arms. She lay resting quietly. They were again with each other. He had not forgotten the time she had protected him from the bear. Keith had tears of remembrance. He was such a young boy, and the bear was so huge, he recalled.

Keith's mother came into the kitchen, and seeing Tina lying on the table and bandaged, she knew the wolf had been hurt. "Frank, will Tina be all right? How did she get hurt?" Ellen asked.

"Yes, I am sure she will recover full use of her paw. We think it was a bear. Probably the same bear that tried to attack Keith and Tina chased off so many years ago."

Keith did not move, and Tina lay quietly in his loving arms, sleeping. Dawn came and Tina awakened and opened her eyes. With gratitude she licked Keith's hand. They were friends together as before. Her pain was gone. The family began to move around and make breakfast. Tina was then able to stand and quietly drank the water Keith gave her. Tina wanted to go back to the wild and her pack. It was her calling.

"Can she go back?" asked Keith.

"Yes, she can," answered his father. "She is able to walk now."

Tina then turned and howled her gratitude. But to everybody's surprise, Silver was quietly waiting outside at the edge of the forest. He wanted to join his mate. Silver returned Tina's call, and she left to join him. Silver had returned to find Tina, his mate, in life or in death. They both silently left, returning to their home, the forest.

Tina was with her pack again. But this was not the end. Keith vowed he would see Tina again. Frank agreed to make the trip with Keith.

"Yes, Keith," Frank Moore told his son. "We will both go to see Tina soon, and she will welcome us again as she did you when you were a young boy."

One such night Keith and Frank Moore rode to the forest, and there in all her majesty was Tina again, waiting for them with her life-long mate, Silver. They both acknowledged Keith and his father and then silently turned and went back into the forest. It had been done. The meeting had been made. Keith was to return again and again to meet his friend Tina and Silver, her mate. The bear that had frightened Keith as such a young boy was gone. It had been trapped by the Indians as a reprisal for eating their crops.

Such was the happy ending for them both. Many times after that, the Indians saw a huge wolf and a man silhouetted against the moon. Together they roamed the forest. The Indians knew it was Tina, the wolf spirit and leader of the pack. She was again with the man she had guarded so well when he was just a boy. Such was their enduring love. The love of the ancient wolf who had bonded with man so long ago and their descendents that today guard us so well. Man will never be alone as he was once in the ancient forests of yesteryear.

Tommy and the Christmas Cat

Chapter One

It was Christmas Eve and Tommy was sleeping in his room. His house in New York was decorated for the holiday. A huge Christmas tree was lit in the living room below. Tommy's parents were sleeping. Tommy knew that Santa Claus would come and leave him the presents he had asked for. The house was quiet and peaceful, waiting for his visit.

Suddenly he heard a strange noise that woke him up. He was surprised to see at his window a lovely white cat with blue eyes. The cat had a collar of sparkling snowflakes. *What would a cat be doing in my room? I must be dreaming,* he thought. Tommy looked at the cat, still sitting at his window.

Tommy asked, "Who are you? What are you doing in my room?"

The cat answered, "I am Snowflake the Cat. I have come from Snowflake Land to see you. We make all the snowflakes that fall from the skies and make your homes so white and beautiful in the winter. My mistress, the Snowflake Queen, has sent me."

Tommy still thought he was dreaming. "I am only a boy. What does your queen want with me?" he asked the beautiful white cat at his window.

"The queen wants you to take home a snowflake baby for everybody to see and love."

"I don't know where Snowflake Land is, and I don't know how to get there," answered Tommy.

"Just follow me and I will take you there," the cat said.

Tommy then joined his friend Snowflake, and together they flew through the blue of the skies, and the pale moon shone upon them. Soon Tommy and Snowflake found themselves in Snowflake Land. Tommy was amazed at its beauty. It was a land of snow white plains and ice palaces of clear crystal.

"I didn't know Snowflake Land was such a beautiful place," Tommy said. "What do you do here, and where is your queen?"

"We make all the snowflakes that drop to your earth and cover it with a beautiful white blanket. It is the snow you like so much to play in," said Snowflake.

"I never knew this before," Tommy said. "I must tell my mother when I go home."

Chapter Two: Tommy and the Jack of Diamonds

Suddenly a new friend appeared. It was the Jack of Diamonds. The Jack was a large, square playing card with red diamonds on the front and back. The Jack had thin legs that were covered by a white cloth sprinkled with red diamonds.

"My friend, Jack, I have brought Tommy here," said Snowflake.

"What took you so long? I have been waiting for you," said Jack.

"Tommy and I had a very pleasant ride sightseeing amongst the stars. The moon was pale yellow and lighted our way," said Snowflake.

Tommy agreed with Snowflake. "Yes, we did. I really liked it," he told Jack.

The Jack told Snowflake, "I have Tommy's magic shoes so he can walk with us to see the queen. I will put them on."

Jack put a dazzling pair of red shoes on Tommy. They were dotted with snowflakes that never melted and glistened in the snow. Then Tommy, the Jack, and Snowflake began walking down the road to see the queen.

Tommy had never seen such a beautiful land. There were ice palaces and monuments of clear ice, one on another, as far as he could see. The three continued walking until they met two white ducks.

"Who are you two, and where are you going?" asked Jack. "I am the Jack of Diamonds and these are my friends Tommy and the cat Snowflake, whose mistress is the Snowflake Queen."

"My name is Donnie and my brother is Dickey. We are pedigreed ducks," Donnie told them.

"What is a pedigreed duck?" asked Jack.

"We are the ducks that fly high and far over Snowflake Land with the queen's snowflake angel. We look over her snowflake babies."

"Do you like to fly?" asked Jack.

"Dickey and I love it. We would not be without flying. The queen appreciates that we fly over the land and watch over her snowflake babies," Donnie said.

"Where are you going?" Dickey asked them.

Jack answered, "We are going to see the Snowflake Queen. She wants to give Tommy a snowflake baby to take home. Would you like to come with us to see her?"

"Yes," the ducks answered.

"Then we shall all go to see the queen."

Then they all walked down the road with Jack to see the queen.

Chapter Three: The Road of the Snowflake Bridge

They all walked down the road of Snowflake Land, alive with sparkling snowflake diamonds. Soon they came to a bridge of snowflakes.

"What shall we do, Jack?" asked Tommy. "Shall we go over the bridge or under it?"

Jack replied, "Never cross a bridge until you come to it. We will go over it."

So the little group—Jack, Tommy, and the two pedigreed ducks, Donnie and Dickey, walked across the bridge until they got to the other side. Snowflake the Cat actually flew across the bridge and waited for them. Yes, this was a cat that could actually fly. They then saw two white mice.

"Mice, what are you doing here?" asked the Jack of Diamonds.

"We are guarding the bridge for the Snowflake Queen," one of the mice answered.

"Why are you guarding the bridge for the Snowflake Queen?" asked Jack.

"We are guarding the bridge for the queen so she may be sure her snowflake babies can safely cross it," the mouse told Jack.

"Mice, what are your names?" asked the Jack of Diamonds.

"My name is Marty and my brother's name is Manny," answered Marty, and Manny nodded in agreement.

"Do you want to go with us to see the queen?" Jack offered.

"Yes, we do," both mice answered.

So off this band of travelers walked: Tommy, the Jack of Diamonds, the two ducks, and now the two white mice, Marty and Manny, who had been guarding the Snowflake Bridge. The queen's cat, Snowflake, romped happily along, playing in the snow as he went.

"Where is the Queen of Snowflake Land?" Tommy asked the Jack of Diamonds."

"The queen is at the Cat's Meow," he answered. "That is where Snowflake, the queen's cat, lives also. We will be there soon. Keep walking," Jack told the group.

So they all kept walking until in front of them was a sparkling lake of ice-blue waters. There were snowflake diamonds glistening as far as the eye could see. It was so beautiful Tommy and the others stood still in awe to see it.

They all walked on in a row. The snow on the ground was soft under their feet. The Jack of Diamonds proudly showed his suit of red diamonds on his card body. Walking was no effort in Snowflake Land. Tommy's red shoes shone as far as the eye could see. The queen's cat, Snowflake, bounded happily in the snow as he went. He purred happily, for he was home at last. Donnie and Dickey, the ducks, and Marty and Manny, the white mice, happily followed them.

Chapter Four: The Ice-Skating Rabbits

In the distance, the group saw an unusual sight. Was it? Could it be? Yes, it was. Two white rabbits skating on the lake. They actually skated over to them.

"My name is Ronnie, and my brother is Rodney," said Ronnie the Rabbit to Jack. "Who are you and why are you here?"

"I am the Jack of Diamonds, special courier of the Snowflake Queen. My friend Tommy, the boy, is from earth," he told Ronnie and Rodney. "Snowflake is the queen's cat, and the ducks are Donnie and Dickey. Our two friends the white mice are Marty and Manny, who guard the Snowflake Bridge for the Snowflake Queen. We are all traveling to see the Snowflake Queen. She is going to give Tommy a snowflake baby to take home."

"What is a snowflake baby?" asked Ronnie and Rodney.

"A snowflake baby is a beautiful baby of snowflakes that fall to the ground each winter when it snows."

"We would like one also. May we have one?" Ronnie asked the Jack of Diamonds.

"Would you and your brother like to come with us?" asked Jack.

Ronnie answered, "We would very much like to come with you. We want to see the Snowflake Queen, and we want a snowflake baby to take back to the lake and skate with us."

"I am sure the queen will grant your request, Ronnie," answered the Jack of Diamonds.

Then the two skaters, Ronnie and Rodney, took off their skates and joined the happy group of travelers who walked on chatting and showing their landmarks to the others.

Chapter Five: The Three Wishes

The Jack of Diamonds said to the group, "The queen of Snowflake Land can grant all of you a special wish for yourselves. Is there anything that you might want?"

Snowflake the Christmas Cat wanted a sister cat to fly with him. "That is my wish," he said.

Donnie and Dickey answered, "We want a special lake that is warm all winter so we may swim all year round. We want to swim with our friends, the ducks and their babes. There should be berries and nuts all the year round for us. Will the queen grant this wish?"

"I am sure the queen will grant your wish," answered the Jack of Diamonds.

"May we have a ball of cheese that we can never finish eating?" asked Marty and Manny. "We would like that very much. We are the guardians of the queen's bridge so her snowflake babies can cross."

"If your wishes are good, the queen will grant them all," answered the Jack of Diamonds. "Your wish is very good to eat," he told Marty and Manny. "The queen appreciates your guarding her bridge so the snowflake babies can pass. I am sure the queen will grant your wishes."

"Thank you," answered the two white mice.

Tommy then asked, "May I have a wish too?"

"Of course you may," answered Jack. "What is your wish?"

Tommy answered, "I wish for a brother I can talk to, for I am so lonely in my room. I was glad Snowflake the Cat visited me."

"You have a good wish. I'm sure the queen will grant it just for you."

Ronnie and Rodney then said, "We would like special ice skates that can fly above the earth and visit the stars and the moon and our friend the sun."

"You two have a wonderful wish. I am sure the queen will grant it,"

Jack told them. "Hurry, let's all of us move on. The queen is waiting for us," he told the group.

The travelers moved on to meet the queen in her palace at Snowflake Land. Suddenly it started to snow.

"We are getting close to the queen's palace; that is why it is snowing. Do you see all the snowflake babies around us?" asked Jack.

Sure enough, tiny hand-sized snowflake babies fell all around them from the sky. What a beautiful sight!

"Keep walking," Jack said to the group. "We are almost there."

Suddenly there appeared to the group a wondrous sight. It was the queen's beautiful palace high in the sky. Tommy and the group of friends looked at this beautiful sight in awe and in silence. The palace was a magnificent design of sculptured ice on designs of all sizes and shapes. Around the palace danced multicolored elves playing on harps of diamond-studded snowflake babies.

Chapter Six: The Snowflake Queen

The group of travelers waited patiently for the queen. Suddenly the elves sounded their trumpets and stood in a row, for the Queen of Snowflake Land had come. There, appearing in all her majesty, was a lovely queen with hair of sparkling snowflakes and eyes the brilliant green of the Snowflake Lakes. After her rode two knights in green attire on their steeds of white. A brilliant sight to behold.

The Jack of Diamonds knelt low. "Your majesty, I am your humble servant. I have brought Tommy here so he may bring your beautiful snowflake baby home as you have asked. I have obeyed your wishes. My dear queen, I humbly present Tommy, the boy from New York, to you."

"Rise, my subject," said the queen to the Jack of Diamonds. "Where is Tommy?"

"Tommy is here beside me, your majesty, beautiful queen," he told her.

Then a lovely voice asked, "Who are you, my son? Are you Tommy?"

"Yes, my name is Tommy of New York. Your cat Snowflake brought me here at your request. I was told I am to bring back a snowflake baby to New York so all the world can see your lovely snowflake babies. The Jack of Diamonds gave me my magic shoes so I could walk on the Snowflake Roads to your palace."

The queen asked Tommy, "Will you take a beautiful snowflake baby home if I ask you to?"

"Yes, I will," said Tommy. "Where are the snowflake babies?"

"I have them in a special place here at the palace. I will give them to you when you go home," said the queen. "Meanwhile, let us celebrate your coming here, for I am jubilant at your arrival. My knights will serve you and Jack and your friends with my special brew to celebrate."

Then the knights served Tommy and his friends the magic brew. They drank until the glasses were empty and all exclaimed they had never had such a good-tasting brew. Surely a drink of queens.

Rodney and Ronnie said, "This is really good. It tastes like cream of lettuce punch. Let's have some more." The knights served them again.

Donnie and Dickey especially enjoyed the punch and asked for more. "It tastes like lake berries," they told the queen. "This is really good." The two white mice enjoyed the drink and also asked for more.

Marty and Manny exclaimed, "This is the best cheese drink we ever had. May we have more?" they asked the knights, who served them again and again. To all of Tommy's friends, the magic punch was their hearts' wishes.

Tommy then said to the queen, "Where is my punch and my friend Jack's punch?"

The queen answered, "I have a special magic brew for you and Jack and my snowflake cat. You will all dream of your heart's delight."

Then Tommy, Jack, and Snowflake the Cat fell into a deep sleep after drinking the magic brew. Tommy had a special dream. He dreamt he was a knight in armor wearing a steel shield and carrying a sword entrusted to him with diamonds and rubies.

Tommy was riding a white stallion and had set out to save the king's daughter Penelope, who had been kidnapped by the robbers of the black knight from the evil forest. Tommy followed the robbers to their camp and rushed in to save Penelope on his stallion, Prince. Then they galloped on Prince's back to Princess Penelope's palace. The king granted Penelope's hand in marriage to Tommy and gave him the title of Prince Thomas, the king-in-waiting, with Penelope to be his queen.

At that Tommy woke up. He noticed the queen, looking very much like Penelope, standing over him and smiling. "Did you like your dream, Tommy?" she asked.

"Very much so," answered Tommy. "I dreamt I was a knight in shining armor, and I saved Penelope, the king's daughter, from the black knight of the evil forest and his bandits. I was knighted Prince Thomas, the king-in-waiting, and Penelope was to be my queen."

Snowflake the Cat told the queen he dreamed of a beautiful white cat named Angela. "Angela was so beautiful. She was almost another star in the heavens," he said. "We flew the heavens and amongst the stars. We had a wonderful flight together. I love her dearly. I want to always be with her."

The Jack of Diamonds was delighted. "I dreamt I was a complete suit of cards that played with all the children in the land. I loved it. Thank you, beloved queen, for that magic brew."

But Tommy knew it was time to go home. He was missing his father and mother. It was Christmas and he knew he should be there with them.

Tommy asked the queen, "May I have the snowflake baby to take home? It is Christmas and I miss my parents. I want to go home."

"Yes, you may," answered the queen. "I know the children of the land will love my beautiful snowflake baby when you bring it home to them in New York."

Tommy kissed the Snowflake Queen good-bye. "I hope to see you next Christmas, dear queen, with Snowflake, your cat."

"You are always welcome at Snowflake Land, dear Tommy," the queen answered him, and returned to her palace with the elves dancing merrily by her side, tumbling and singing, and her knights following her.

Then Tommy tearfully said good-bye to his new friends.

"Good-bye, dear Donnie and Dickey, my pedigreed duck friends. I will miss you both. I will come back next Christmas with our friend Snowflake and the Jack of Diamonds, who will be by then a whole suit of cards."

Tommy embraced his friends Manny and Marty, the white mice. "I am so glad I met you two. I will never forget you. Good-bye just for now. I love you both," he said as he waved good-bye.

Then, tearfully, Tommy said good-bye to Ronnie and Rodney, the skating rabbits. "I will be back to see you again next year, and we will skate together as we always have with our friend the Jack of Diamonds."

Tommy and Snowflake flew swiftly to earth, for it was Christmas Eve. It was time for Santa Claus to come to the house as he always had each year.

Tommy wanted to see his mother and father, and his wish came true. He opened his eyes and saw his smiling father and beautiful mother.

"Merry Christmas, Tommy. Come downstairs and see the presents Santa Claus has left you under the tree."

Tommy went down the stairs and saw the presents under the tree. The talking robot he had asked for was there. There was a wooden train to pull with his friends, a racing car set, and a city to run it in.

Tommy wondered where the queen's snowflake babies were. He looked out the window of the living room, and there the snowflake babies were, coming down as beautiful as beautiful could be. It was Christmas and it was the first snow of the season. Tiny little snowflake babies were laughing and spinning in the air—a beautiful gift from the Queen of Snowflake Land.

"Mother," said Tommy, "the Snowflake Queen has kept her promises. Her snowflake babies are all outside. They are all over and around our house. Mother, they are so beautiful. Come to the window and see them."

"Tommy, what Snowflake Queen are you talking about?" She asked.

"The Queen of Snowflake Land. Last night when I went to sleep, Snowflake, her cat, came into my room. We went to Snowflake Land to see the queen, who wanted me to bring back to earth a beautiful snowflake baby for all the world to see. I met the Jack of Diamonds, who gave me special shoes to wear so I could walk in Snowflake Land with him to see the queen.

"Donnie and Dickey, the pedigreed ducks, also came with us to see the queen. I met Marty and Manny, the white mice who guard the Snowflake Bridge for the queen. Then my good friends Ronnie and Rodney, the skating rabbits, also came with my friend the Jack of Diamonds. We all traveled through beautiful Snowflake Land to see the queen. The queen wanted to give me a beautiful snowflake baby to take back to earth for everyone on earth to see how beautiful they are. It was her special gift to us here."

"Tommy, you have been dreaming," his mother told him.

"I guess you are right, Mother," Tommy said. "You are always right."

"I'm glad you think so, Tommy. You make me a very happy mother," she answered.

Then Tommy knew he had woken up from a wonderful dream. He had gone to Snowflake Land and met the Queen of Snowflake Land. Snowflake, her cat, who was in his room, and the Jack of Diamonds had been waiting for him, and when he put on his magic shoes they went to see the queen.

What a lovely land he had walked through with the pedigreed ducks, the white mice, and the skating rabbits. The Jack of Diamonds had led them to the beautiful queen's palace. What a beautiful sight of sculptured ice.

"Mother, I will wait for Christmas next year and for Snowflake the Cat to take me again to Snowflake Land to see our beloved queen again," Tommy said.

"Christmas is another year away," said his mother. "You may very well have the brother you always wanted by then. Would you like that, Tommy?"

"I would love that," he told her.

Tommy's father agreed. "Yes, you may very well have the brother you have wanted for so long. Merry Christmas, Tommy."

His father and mother gave him an affectionate hug and kiss for Christmas morning.

"The snowflake babies are falling all around us, and they are so beautiful. You must thank the queen when you see her again," Tommy's mother told him. "May we all have a happy and loving New Year. Let's have breakfast, for we have a lot of people who will visit us this special day, and we surely must go to see them too. It's the most wonderful day of the year, next to your birthday," she said, and his father agreed.

Then they ate their Christmas breakfast, and Tommy gave his mother her Christmas present—a lovely embroidered handkerchief—and his father a blue tie, his favorite color. The day went by swiftly, and many friends and fond relatives came to their house to celebrate with them on this special day. The evening was spent visiting family and friends they had known for many a Christmas.

But all good times go by swiftly, and soon it was time to say good-bye.

"Merry Christmas, dear children, to you from all of us."

"May there be many more of this beautiful day for us to celebrate."

"This is surely the special day of giving and loving for us all."

"Merry Christmas, children. St. Nicholas will soon be at your house."

"Good-bye for now. I'll see you next year. Until then, I love you all."

"Merry Christmas and a full and happy New Year!"

Squeaky the Squirrel

The forest of East Haven was turning gold and red. The birds were flying south for the winter, and cool winds nestled in the meadows and hills. Nature was at its best and beautiful in its autumn glory.

All was not well in the squirrel and chipmunk families of East Haven. Squeaky the Squirrel and Tommy the Chipmunk and their families were running out of food. Their babes were hungry in their nests. Oh, poor babes.

Squeaky, the head of the squirrel families, had been watching over the meadows. He saw clearly who the villain was. It was Sam the Skunk, who was eating their food and growing fat and warm for the winter. Meanwhile the squirrel and chipmunk families were hungry and getting hungrier. Their acorns and berries were slowly but surely disappearing. Their babes were crying in their nests. What to do? What to do? Soon the harsh winter would be coming.

Squeaky and Tommy held a conference and decided to talk to Sam, the culprit skunk.

"Everybody is welcome to talk to Sam," said Squeaky and Tommy. "Come with us, Sam is in the meadow right now eating our food. Hurry, let's go," they said to their families.

The squirrel families and chipmunk families followed them—all but one little squirrel whose name was Scotty. He ran back and forth looking out at everything. The two families made Scotty the lookout. He was small and not easily seen.

Finally under Scotty's direction they assembled in the meadow to talk to the culprit, Sam the Skunk. They saw Sam, as big as life, munching on the acorns and berries they so badly needed to eat with their babes in the winter months.

Squeaky called for the squirrels and chipmunks to assemble and talk to Sam the Skunk. They all advanced in the meadow to see him. The rabbits and birds curiously watched in amazement. Dozens of squirrels and chipmunks were advancing on a lone skunk in the meadow. Whatever would they do to him?

The squirrel and chipmunk families were going to talk to Sam about their food supply and ask him to stop eating it. Surely they would be hungry that winter if Sam didn't. Bad Sam, he was eating all their food.

The skunk heard them and turned in surprise. What a sight. He was surrounded by dozens of squirrels and chipmunks.

"Stop eating our food or we will go hungry this winter. Our babes in their nests are hungry too. Don't you realize you are eating our food?" Squeaky and Tommy said to Sam.

Sam the Skunk said to Squeaky and Tommy, "I didn't know you saw me."

"We had to. You were in plain sight, eating in the meadow. Don't you know it is wrong to take something that is not yours? The acorn and berries are for all of us. Why did you do this?"

"I didn't think of it that way. Besides, I didn't think anybody was watching me," said Sam.

"Stop eating our food and we will forgive you," Squeaky and Tommy said to Sam.

"I am sorry I took your food," said Sam. "I won't take all the food anymore. On my honor I will not eat all the food again. I apologize to the squirrel and chipmunk families. I am truly sorry for what I did."

"Your apology is accepted," Squeaky and Tommy answered. "Now we can all live in peace again."

The winds grew colder and the days shorter. Suddenly there were white dots on the ground. They covered the green limbs of the forest trees. The first snow had fallen. A beautiful white blanket covered the forest. Solid white crystals of ice decorated the trees.

The animals of the forest were happily anticipating their annual visit from Santa Claus. They expressed their joy by decorating the trees with gifts of berries, and the babes of the forest left nuts for him.

Suddenly in the distance they heard the tinkle of bells and the clatter of small hooves. The animals of the forest waited expectantly. Was it true? Yes, it was. Santa Claus was coming to their forest. Then, there in their sight, were the reindeer and Santa's sled, just brimming with presents. At last the jolly elf had come. But what was this? There was another visitor with him. Could it be? Yes, it was. Mrs. Claus had come this time with him. She was jolly and red in her attire. What rejoicing rang through the forest.

Both Mr. and Mrs. Claus had arrived in their sled, with the reindeer leading the way. Their bright red sled carried goodies for all the forest animals, especially the babes of the forest. Sam the Skunk, now reformed and forgiven, waited for his gifts also. The sled carrying Mr. and Mrs. Claus was just brimming with presents.

Mr. and Mrs. Claus proceeded to give their presents to one and all. The babes of the forest were given cherry fruits, and spiced sugar apples were given to all. Sam the Skunk loved the butter popcorn he received. What a treat!

Mr. and Mrs. Claus swung merrily to the tune of jingle bells, and the forest animals danced with them. What a sight to see! What joy was had by all!

Then with a quick turn Mr. and Mrs. Claus mounted their sled and sped into the night with their reindeer. The moon shone brightly on them, and the stars of the night twinkled.

Santa Claus addressed the animals of the forest before they left. "My wife, Mrs. Claus, and I are here to wish all of you a very special Christmas and a wonderful New Year. We have other forests to visit and other friends to see. Stay well and we will both be back next year. Merry, merry Christmas and a very happy New Year."

They then sped on in the night of their yearly visit, waving to all as they passed high into the starry skies. "Merry Christmas to you children, and a happy New Year."

Ronnie the Rabbit and the Christmas Gift

Ronnie the Rabbit was walking around the lake eating carrots from Mrs. Goode's yard when he came upon his friend Slippery the Fish. Poor Slippery was floundering on the grass, gasping for air.

"Ronnie, please help me. I must get back into the water or I will drown in the air," he gasped. "I can't breathe. If you help me get back into the water, I will tell you a secret I have known for a long time."

"I will help you get back into the water, my friend, but what is this secret of yours?" Ronnie asked.

"There is a treasure chest of gold left by Simon the Pirate under the elm tree. Simon never came back for it. His ship was wrecked on the rocks in a storm."

"What?" asked Ronnie. "Are you really sure?"

"I am positive," Slippery told Ronnie. "My grandfather Sam watched him bury the chest when he was swimming past the old elm tree by the lake many years ago. You must push me back into the water or I will drown in the air. One, two, three. Now push!"

Ronnie gently pushed Slippery back into the water and watched him swim away. Then he went to the old elm tree. "Is this true what Slippery said?" Ronnie said to himself. "How can I get Simon the Pirate's chest out from under the elm tree? Christmas is coming and I want to give the gold to the poor children and their families of the lake. I am afraid they won't have any presents this year if I don't."

While Ronnie was figuring out how to get the pirate's chest from out of the ground under the elm tree, he heard a familiar voice.

"My friend, why are you so puzzled?"

Ronnie turned and there was his friend Pete the Possum nestled in the grass.

"Pete, my friend, I am so glad to see you. I need your help. I don't know how I can get Simon the Pirate's chest of gold from under the elm tree. He buried it many years ago and never came back for it."

"Why didn't Simon come back for his gold?" Pete asked.

Ronnie said, "Slippery the Fish told me he was shipwrecked on the rocks in the inlet in a storm and never came back."

"Poor, poor Simon. I feel so sorry for him," Pete said. "I will help you, Ronnie. I will dig it up with my claws. They are sharp and strong."

But unknown to Ronnie and Pete, Sylvester the Snake was watching, and he suddenly slithered up, stinging his tail.

"No. I won't let you dig that chest of gold up. I am mean and ornery, and I don't want the children of the lake to have any Christmas presents."

"What shall we do now?" asked Ronnie. But before Pete could answer, a small dog appeared on the scene.

"Is there a problem? You two look like you are lost. What happened?" Buddy, their friend the dog, asked them.

"Yes, we have a problem," Ronnie answered. "Sylvester the Snake frightened us with his stinging tail. He won't let us dig under the elm tree for the chest of gold Simon the Pirate left there after he was lost in a storm. That is what Slippery the Fish told us. We want to give the gold to the poor children of the lake for their Christmas present. I fear they will not have any Christmas presents this year if we can't dig up Simon's chest of gold. What shall we do, Buddy?"

"Never fear, I will help you," Buddy told Ronnie. "I will bark at Sylvester when he tries to stop you and Pete from digging up the pirate's chest of gold. I want to help the poor children of the lake get Christmas presents too."

The three of them went cautiously back to the elm tree, for Sylvester was still silently waiting in the grass to stop them. They surrounded him, and Buddy's loud barking woke the snake up. Sylvester the Snake slithered off, frightened by the dog's loud barking.

At last now they could begin digging for the chest. All three dug and carried the grass from under the elm tree to the lake so the children could use it to fish on. What a happy hour. It went by so quickly.

"We must hurry. It is getting dark and we won't be able to dig much longer," said Ronnie.

They all continued to dig more quickly, and suddenly there was a very loud clang!

"It is true!" exclaimed Ronnie. "It really is buried here. We have found Simon's gold chest. Slippery the Fish was right!"

After the trio of friends rested, Buddy the Dog got a rope from his backyard, and they wrapped the rope around the pirate's chest and pulled.

"One, two, three. Now pull," Ronnie told them. Up came the pirate's chest. But what to do with it? they asked themselves. How would they open it now that they had it?

"We will take it to Mayor Frank. He will know what to do with it. He will know how to open it, I am sure," Ronnie told them.

Meanwhile Sylvester the Snake crawled back to watch them. "I heard what you said. You have found the chest of Simon's gold. I am mean and ornery. I won't let you give it to the poor children of the lake. I am going to wrap myself around the chest so you can't have it."

"No, you won't," said Ronnie. "Buddy won't let you."

Buddy barked fiercely at Sylvester, who slithered off, a very frightened snake. While Buddy pulled the rope and Pete pushed the chest, they managed with much effort to get it to Mayor Frank's office, where a very surprised secretary was waiting for them.

The secretary immediately went to get Mayor Frank. "Mayor Frank, there is a strange chest outside with the letter 'S' on it. A dog, a rabbit, and a possum have brought it here. I believe they are waiting for you," she told the mayor.

Mayor Frank came out to see the chest and the animal friends who had brought it to his office. "Good heavens!" he exclaimed when he saw the letter "S" on the chest. "It's the chest Simon the Pirate left here many years ago. Simon's boat sank, and no one has seen him since. My grandfather told me about this when I was just a young boy. Nobody has been able to find it until now.

"Christmas is coming. With your permission, Buddy, Pete, and Ronnie, I shall give the gold to the poor children of the lake. May I?" he asked the three friends. "They will have a Merry Christmas too."

"Yes, you have our permission." Buddy, Pete, and Ronnie all agreed it was a wonderful idea.

The mayor took his keys and one by one he used them to try to open the chest. None worked until he tried an old and rusted key his grandfather had given him many years ago. The key snapped open the chest.

"I have found the key!" he exclaimed. "I never knew where Simon's chest was until now."

Truly, it was the chest of gold coins Simon the Pirate had left but never returned to claim. The shiny gold coins had not aged. They were just waiting to be given to the poor children of the lake and their families.

"What a wonderful Christmas the poor children of the lake will have with their families too," the mayor told the three friends.

They all thrilled to the idea.

The secretary said she would tell the children of the lake of their unexpected gift for Christmas. "I will tell the children that thanks to Ronnie and his friends Pete and Buddy, they are going to have a very merry Christmas this year." She left to tell the children of the lake and their families.

Suddenly, without warning, there was a clatter of hooves and a hearty voice exclaiming, "Merry Christmas to all. I am here from the North Pole with presents for all of you. I will leave them under the Christmas tree at the mayor's office.

"What's this? A chest with an 'S' on it? Whose chest is it?" a surprised Santa Claus asked Mayor Frank.

The mayor explained, "It is the chest of Simon the Pirate, who was lost at sea many years ago. It was hidden under the elm tree, and Ronnie the Rabbit, Pete the Possum, and Buddy the Dog found it and brought it to my office. Now the poor children of the lake and their families will have presents for Christmas."

"Wonderful!" Santa exclaimed. "Are these the three friends here?"

"Yes," the mayor told Santa Claus.

Santa told the three friends, "I have special presents for our animal friends. Bones that last all year for Buddy the friendly dog, and a head of lettuce that never is finished for Ronnie the Rabbit, and Pete the Possum and his friends will have carrots that last all year."

They were very happy animals. They all sent their regards to Mrs. Claus and the elves who make all the toys for Santa Claus and his trip Christmas Eve to the children of the world. They told Santa Claus they would be especially waiting for him next year also.

"I have to go now," Santa said. "I have a lot to do this year. Good-bye for now, and merry Christmas till next year, when we meet again. I will give your regards to Mrs. Claus and the elves. They are busy right now making the children's toys for next year."

Santa Claus mounted his sleigh and joined his trusty reindeers. With a wave good-bye he sped into the starry sky.

"Merry Christmas to all until we meet next year. Stay safe," he called out to them. It was truly a merry Christmas for the children of the lake and all the children of the world.

Blackie the Hero Cat

Chapter One: The Story of a Boy and His Cat

Blackie the Kitten was sleeping peacefully in his soft bed by the Barton's Christmas tree. Blackie was a gift from Grandmother Barton to her family. He was a beautiful black kitten for all of them to love. The other members of the family were visiting with their guests, and the door to the house was always being opened and shut.

Blackie, curious as all little kittens are, thought to himself, *What is outside, and what are those white specks out there? I'll just go out and see.*

Blackie was close to the door, and when it opened again, he darted past the family and ran curiously outside. Poor Blackie. It was really cold. He had found himself in a blinding snowstorm.

"Good heavens, it is so cold out here. My paws hurt, and the white specks are getting in my eyes. I can't see. Oh, I wish I were inside." Then Blackie curled up in a ball and cried, "Meow! Meow! Somebody please find me. I will surely freeze out here!"

But Blackie's cries did not go unanswered. Suddenly he heard clump, clump, clump. Somebody was walking towards him.

"I hope I get found. I am so cold and wet," cried little Blackie.

A man passing by had heard the kitten and looked down. "Kitten, what are you doing out here? Don't you know it's snowing and no place for a kitten or anybody?"

Blackie was only a kitten and did not know. He was very cold, and when the man swooped him up in his arms, he meowed contentedly. The man snuggled wet and cold Blackie under his coat. He was now safe and warm.

"Who left you out here?" the man said to him. But Blackie did not answer. He meowed contentedly and fell asleep, just happy to be held.

"I will take you home to my son, Kevin. You are just what he wants for Christmas," said the man.

Again Blackie meowed contentedly, for he was warm and safe with this man. Off the two went in the snow. When the man opened the door to his house, he called to his son. "Merry Christmas, Kevin. I have a big surprise for you!"

"Merry Christmas, Father. Mother has made a special dinner for us."

Kevin's mother kissed them both, wishing them a merry Christmas.

In his father's arms was the most beautiful black kitten Kevin ever saw.

"Daddy, is the kitten for me?"

"Yes, it is for you. You can have him if you take good care of him. I found him shivering in the snow. Somebody didn't take care of him. He is ours now. Do you want to hold him?"

"Oh, Daddy, yes I do!" Kevin gently held the sleepy but warm Blackie in his arms. "Thank you," he said. "I will watch over him always. I will love him, and he will be mine. I am so happy to have him."

Kevin's mother made a special Christmas dinner for them, and Blackie was given a special treat of fish, which he loved and purred in contentment after eating. Resting happily in Kevin's arms after being rescued from a cold, wintry night, Blackie was the happiest of kittens. The lost kitten had been found by a loving family that really wanted him. The lost can always be found by the ones who love them.

Kevin told his father, "This is the happiest Christmas of my life. I have Blackie now. Why would someone let Blackie go in a snowstorm?"

"Some people are not careful of the ones they love and find someday they have lost them," his father said. "But happily for us, we have Blackie now, and you and he will be together for many years.

"We all have to go to bed now, for tomorrow is another day, and Christmas will be here soon. There will be other presents from Santa

Claus, and maybe he has brought this year the bicycle you wanted for so long."

Kevin kissed his parents good night.

"We must always remember the less fortunate this time of year and share our blessings with them."

"I promise, Father, I will remember." Then Kevin carried sleepy Blackie to his room and placed him under the covers with him.

Chapter Two: Blackie Saves Kevin

This was the start of a lifelong friendship. They shared many hours of enjoyment together. When Kevin fished at the lake, he always took Blackie with him. While Kevin was growing up, they were always together. Kevin was true to the promise he had made his father and looked out for Blackie.

One summer's day, as Kevin was leaving the lake to go home, he stumbled over a small rock. "I hurt my ankle," he said to Blackie. "Go home, Blackie," and he motioned him to their house. Blackie instantly obeyed.

Blackie ran as fast as his four paws could carry him. He knew Kevin needed help. Over the lawns he ran and meowed loudly when he got to the house. Kevin's mother heard him and came to the door. When she saw Blackie was alone, she was very alarmed. She knew something had happened to Kevin. They were always together at the lake.

Kevin's mother followed Blackie to the lake and found her son sitting on the grass with what she knew was a sprained ankle.

"Mother, I am so glad to see you. I stumbled and hurt my ankle. I knew Blackie would get you. He is the best cat a boy could have. I love him," he told her.

"I will help you to the house, Kevin, where I will bandage your ankle and call the doctor. You must be more careful when you run or this will happen again to you."

At the house, his mother wrapped Kevin's sprained ankle and called the doctor, who made haste in coming.

"You're lucky this time, Kevin. You could have broken your ankle. Promise your mother and I you will be more careful," he told Kevin. "Just rest for a few weeks and you will be like new." He then went back to his office.

Kevin stayed up in his room and read and kept up with his homework, which one of his teachers had left. She also spoke to Kevin and told him how important it was to be more careful and to run slowly.

A very contented Blackie curled up on the foot of his bed, dreaming happily of the fish in the lake jumping up out of the water. Kevin's mother came and sat by the bed, doing her knitting and serving him delicious meals on a tray. Kevin's father came in every night from work to talk to him about his work at the factory he owned. Kevin enjoyed hearing about it.

The day came when the bandage came off and Kevin's ankle was well again. Being the boy he was, down again to the lake Kevin and Blackie went. Friends for life were these two. A boy and his cat. Happy and free, he and Blackie enjoyed fishing for small sunnies and feeding their friends, the birds and ducks of the lake. Blackie was always with Kevin. They were friends for life.

Blackie was more than a friend; he was the hero of Kevin's family since helping Kevin when he sprained his ankle. Mother fed Blackie very special portions of fish, which he loved. Blackie was petted daily by the family, and he curled at night by Kevin's father's feet, close to the fireplace, contentedly sleeping.

"Well, little fella, I am glad I found you in that snowstorm. Kevin loves you, and you helped my son when he needed you. You are always welcome in my house," he said and then petted him till Blackie fell asleep in his arms.

"Kevin, Christmas will be here soon. Santa Claus will arrive in his special sleigh with all of his reindeer and with presents for all of us and especially for the children."

Kevin wanted a very special gift this year. It was the bicycle he had always wanted, with a bike basket for Blackie to ride in.

Kevin asked his father, "Oh, Daddy, do you think Santa Claus will bring the bicycle I have wanted for so long so Blackie and I can ride around the lake with it? I promise to be careful and ride only on the sidewalk."

"Santa Claus knows you are a good boy. We will see if he brings you the bicycle you want this year," Kevin's father told him. "Meanwhile, merry Christmas from your mother and I, Kevin. Soon Christmas day will be here, and the house will be full of many old friends and relatives and some very special new friends also."

Yes, Christmas day would be soon be there, and Kevin anxiously waited for the moment he would know if Santa had left the wonderful present of his new bicycle.

Chapter Three: Christmas Day

What happiness was through the house that Christmas morning. Kevin came down the stairs to see the most beautifully decorated tree in the whole world, and yes, by the side of the tree was the treasured bicycle Santa Claus had left for him alone.

Kevin's father and mother embraced Kevin while Blackie purred happily at their feet.

"Merry Christmas, Kevin. Santa has been here and left you the bicycle you have wanted for so long. Mother and I are very happy for you. We left Santa some of Mother's gingerbread cookies and milk. I can see he has eaten them. It's a long trip, bringing the children of the world their Christmas presents on Christmas Eve."

Kevin agreed. "Oh, Father and Mother, the bicycle is so beautiful, and there is a bike basket for Blackie. Merry Christmas to you both. I love you so much and Blackie does too. I promise I will only ride on the sidewalk, and I will lend my friends the bicycle too. Some of them don't have bicycles."

"Yes, Kevin, we must share our blessings with others," his father told him.

Then Blackie meowed loudly, and soon he had a gift. It was a ball of his favorite fish-flavored popcorn.

Christmas day was exciting. The children made a snowman with two chestnuts for eyes and a carrot nose. There was a cap for his head. Their sleds bounded down the hills until they were exhausted.

The feast at the Christmas dinner was deliciously good. When their guests finished eating, they gave each other their gifts and spoke happily of other Christmas days long gone. Many old friendships were then renewed, and they were always looking to the next Christmas not too far away. But Christmas day sped by so fast, and it was time to leave and go to their homes before they hardly realized it.

"Merry Christmas and a full and happy New Year, Kevin. We will be all together next year," their friends and family told him.

The guests then left, after bidding good-bye to Kevin's father and mother. They were off to home before dark in the snow of the Christmas holiday. What a wonderful ending to one of the most precious days of the year.

Chapter Four: The Family Down the Road

Christmas day was ending, and Kevin's family and guests went to their homes happy and united once again. Then at last Kevin's father spoke seriously to him.

"Kevin, I know a family not too far from here but down the road who are not as fortunate as we are," he said. "They also have children. I have some presents for them. Would you like to come and help me give them out?"

"Yes, I would be happy to give them their Christmas presents. I would like to meet them also," Kevin told his father. "Mother, may I bring my Monopoly game?"

"Of course you can, Kevin. I am sure they would like to play that game with you. Wish them a merry Christmas for me, will you?"

"Yes, I will, Mother," he told her.

Then Kevin's father put the presents and food in the truck and drove Kevin down a different road to a poorer neighborhood that Kevin had never been in before.

Kevin's father knocked on the door of the old wooden frame house. A lovely lady came to the door with a beautiful baby in her arms.

"Merry Christmas, señora," he said. "Kevin and I have brought some Christmas presents for yourself, your husband, and your children. This is my son, Kevin. May we come in?"

"Welcome to my house," the lovely señora told them. Then her husband, Joseph, came to the door and greeted them. With him were two boys eager to see the new visitors to their home.

"My family and I welcome you," Joseph told Kevin and his father. "May this blessed Yuletide season bring you much love. I am truly blessed you are here with us."

Then Kevin and his father went inside and gave the food and presents to them. There was milk for the new baby and warm clothing for the children and Joseph and his wife, Maria. The children especially liked Kevin and thanked him for his Monopoly game. Kevin promised to come back some rainy day and play it with them.

Then Kevin's father spoke seriously. "Joseph, you have a job with me Monday morning delivering my machinery to my customers."

"Thank you, señor. My family and I will always be grateful for this and in your service. I will be there Monday without fail," Joseph told Kevin's father.

Then as it got to be dark, Kevin and his father made the trip home. They wished the Lopez family a merry Christmas and a very happy

New Year, happy they had done something in the Yule season for the less fortunate. They were very happy at the least for this wonderful holiday.

When Kevin's mother greeted them at the door, she asked, "Kevin, did you and your father enjoy your visit?"

"Yes, Mother, very much. I met the nicest boys. I am going back to play Monopoly with them some rainy day."

Blackie purred contentedly. Kevin was again home.

Then Kevin's father spoke seriously. "I took you to the Lopez family because I wanted you to remember we must always share our good fortune with others less fortunate than ourselves. We are all not as blessed as we are today, Kevin."

"I will remember, Father. When can we go back? I want to play Monopoly with the two Lopez boys. I want them to ride my new bicycle and meet Blackie."

"We can go back very soon. Now we will have some of that turkey left from Christmas day," Kevin's father told him.

After finishing supper, a sleepy-eyed Kevin went to his room to sleep. His father told him, "Tomorrow is another day. Be up early and we will do some more Christmas visiting. Let's really enjoy the season."

They certainly did, going up and down on the town roads visiting friends and children with a fine greeting. "Merry Christmas! This is for you." It was the happiest day for them both.

Then the darkness fell and Kevin's mother served dinner and Blackie curled around Kevin's feet. He told his mother of their visits to the neighbors and their children. She enjoyed every minute of it.

A very sleepy Kevin went up to his room. He said his evening prayers and was thankful for the wonderful day of Christmas and his fine family and Blackie, his cat. He also hoped the Lopez family could share in the wonderful gifts as he and his family did. He kissed his father and mother good night and then they went to their room.

Such was the end of a beautiful Christmas day. Blackie curled in his soft cat bed and slept soundly at the foot of Kevin's bed.

The new day came, and Kevin and his father again visited his employees with presents and news of work. There were many happy people amongst them.

The Lopez family and their boys were not forgotten. Kevin spent many winter nights playing the Monopoly game with them, Blackie curiously looking on.

In the spring they took turns riding Kevin's bike and always on the sidewalk. What spring fun they had.

Kevin and his father became known for their goodwill in the area. Many a merry Christmas was made merrier by these two, the father and son team of Kevin and his dad.

Chapter Five: Blackie the Family Hero

Blackie was adored by Kevin's family from when he was brought as a kitten from a snowstorm. The mother fed him the choicest of cat foods since he had rescued Kevin when he sprained his ankle. Blackie appreciated the attention he got. He purred his contentment to all present whenever he could.

Blackie lived for many years in the household of Kevin and his family. He was loved by everyone. When Kevin went to school, Blackie waited by the living room window for him to come home. As all cats do, he knew the time Kevin would come home. It is a special gift cats have.

They romped and played in the yard for hours, Blackie fetching and finding balls that Kevin hid from him. Blackie had a keen sense of smell. The friends from the house down the road also came to play with Kevin's cat. They played hide and go seek, and Blackie always found the boy or girl who was hiding.

Many a day Kevin's friends asked him, "We are having so much fun—can we stay just a little longer?"

"I will ask my mother if you can stay over and have her delicious pancakes for breakfast."

"Yes," his mother always replied, "yes, you may stay in the guest room and I will make pancakes for breakfast."

A wonderful breakfast was had by all the children. They went home full and happy that next morning.

Blackie lived for many years and had a host of kittens that guarded their neighbors' houses. Many times the Lopez boys came over, and they played in the yard with Blackie and Kevin and took turns riding Kevin's bicycle, always on the sidewalk.

They were good children and grew into beautiful manhood. With the help of Kevin's father, both Lopez boys went to college. They in turn gave packages to the poor at Christmas. A wonderful blessing had been passed down to them.

"Merry Christmas" was heard many times for many years in the house of Kevin and his father. Blackie was well loved by the family, the homeless orphan of the storm found by Kevin's caring father.

Nobody is ever really lost. There is someone somewhere who is waiting for them.

Kevin's father would say to Blackie, "You are always welcome in my house. Merry Christmas, Blackie." Then Blackie purred his version of "Merry Christmas" back.

Peggy the Penguin

Chapter One: The Ice Cavern

Peggy was a happy penguin living in the frozen land of Alaska, which suited her and her family of penguins. The snow was always there for her to play in, and she fished in the cold ocean waters. Many a day she set out to walk through the ice hills and snow of her home to catch fish, her favorite food.

One such day Peggy decided to go for her usual walk, and while alone and not watching, she slid down the slippery side of an ice cavern and found herself alone far below.

"What to do? What to do? Oh, what shall I do?" cried poor, lost Peggy. "I am all alone down here. Nobody can see me."

Suddenly, help arrived in the form of a sled driver and his dogs on the way to Nome, their home. The dogs were beautiful, strong animals that could help save Peggy. She heard the sound of many dogs barking, especially Buddy, the lead dog, who sensed there was somebody below in the ice cavern.

"Oh, help me, please help me," she cried out. Buddy's keen sense of smell told him she was there, and he pointed the sled to the ice cavern. Then Tom, the driver, went to see what was below and saw poor, lost Peggy.

"Good heavens, Buddy, a penguin is in the cavern. We must help her out or she will freeze down there. I will tie this rope around you and throw it down to her so you can pull her up," Tom told his lead dog.

Buddy barked and the rope was thrown down to Peggy. She grabbed the rope with her broad beak and hung on for dear life. Then the powerful dog, with the rope tied to his chest, pulled the rope and pulled poor, lost Peggy to safety.

Peggy told the friendly sled driver, "Oh, thank you for saving me. It was so cold and dark down there, I was afraid I would freeze. Your dog is wonderful. I can't thank him enough. I want to go home now."

Tom replied, "How would you like to come with me and see the rest of the world beyond Alaska? I want to take you to Ocean World, a water resort just full of penguins like yourself. I am sure they would like to see you. They have many visitors at Ocean World to see how beautiful you are."

"Where is Ocean World?"

"It is where I live. Will you go there with me?" Tom asked Peggy.

"Is Ocean World far?"

"Not too far. We will go in the airplane bird that flies high in the skies," Tom explained. Then he took Peggy in his sled and they proceeded to the airport to fly to Tom's home in the United States. He intended to take Peggy to Ocean World so that everybody could see how beautiful Peggy the Penguin really was.

They both boarded the plane, and the stewardess gave Peggy ice water for the trip. The crew was delighted to have a penguin on board. When they landed, Peggy was amazed at the sight of the airport and wanted to know what the sleds with wheels were.

Tom said, "They are automobiles, and they will take us to Ocean World. We will be there very soon."

During her first ride in an automobile, Peggy saw houses. "What are they? I never saw those where I live. We have ice caverns," she told Tom.

Tom answered, "They are the houses we all live in. We stay indoors when it is cold and sometimes inside when it is hot in the summer. We are not like you. You are very lucky. Your home in Alaska is very rich in beauty."

Finally Tom and Peggy arrived at Ocean World, the playground and home of the sea world animals. What a surprise Peggy had. All the animals of the sea were there. They all were waiting for Peggy, for Tom had told Ocean World his penguin friend Peggy was coming. They greeted Peggy with a rousing shout. She flapped her wings. Peggy loved the attention.

"Where is my family, the penguins?" she asked Tom.

"They have a special home at Ocean World, and they all are waiting for you. Do you want to see them now?"

"Yes, I want to see my family," she answered.

Off Tommy and Peggy went to see her family and Peggy's new home at Ocean World. When they arrived, her family of penguins flapped their fins and danced in the aisles, for Peggy was one of them. They were delighted to see her and wanted her to join them. Peggy also flapped her wings and flew right into her new home where all the penguins lived. The long trip had made her lonely.

She was also hungry from the trip and she ate of the fish she had been fed and drank the cold, clear water that was in the lake surrounding their home of stones from Alaska. Then she decided to say good-bye to her friend Tom. She also flapped her wings. Tom knew she meant to stay with the other penguins, and he spoke to her before he left.

"Peggy, you are beautiful. You belong with the penguins, for they are your family. The people of Ocean World will come to see you and admire you and your family. I must go back to my home now, but I will always remember and love you for the lovely creature you are. Good-bye for now. I will always come back to see you," he said to them all. "Be happy and well in your new home at Ocean World."

The people came from all over to see Peggy the Penguin, who had been saved from the frozen depths of an ice cavern. She was a popular celebrity and an immediate success at Ocean World. The visitors flocked to see her, and when they came, Peggy and the penguins put on a show for them in their arena. The visitors loved it. Tom was thought of as a hero.

Peggy enjoyed performing and was delighted to see all the visitors. But she was getting lonely for her home and family in Alaska, and she wanted to go home where she had grown up. One night when only the stars were in sight and Ocean World park was still, Peggy made a foolish move. She flapped her wings and flew away to the land she missed and the family she loved. But unfortunately she was not sure where Alaska was.

Up, up, and away she bravely flew. No other penguin at the park had ever done this before. Peggy flew tirelessly but was not sure where Alaska was. She was determined, however, to get there. On and on lost Peggy flew. Suddenly she found herself in a raging blizzard.

"Oh, I am so cold and tired. I am sorry I left Ocean World. I am hungry too. Maybe I should go back. I am still not home. It is farther than I thought," she realized.

But she could not go back. She was in a blinding winter blizzard. On this freezing cold night she shivered and flew on. She was very tired and cold when she saw a house with the lights still on.

I must stop and take a rest, she thought. *I am sure the owners will not mind.* And she flew onto the roof.

Peggy perched on the roof and nestled by the warm chimney, and she realized how hungry she was. By then she also knew she was lost. Poor, poor Peggy.

Maybe that was not such a good idea, leaving Ocean World and not telling anyone where I was going. I didn't know Alaska was so far away. I wish someone would come and find me, Peggy thought. *What is this warm thing I feel beside me?* As she was looking down the warm chimney, she suddenly found herself falling. Then she felt something hot and scrambled out of the way. She had fallen into a fireplace. When she looked around, she found herself in a large room with a green tree and twinkling lights.

Where am I? she thought. *Could I be home in Alaska? I never saw this before in Alaska.*

But Peggy wasn't home in Alaska. It was Christmas Eve and she was in the home of Chris and Amy, two children waiting for the Christmas Eve visit of Santa Claus. Peggy was very hungry and ate the cookies they had left him and drank the milk. She was sleepy and lay down to rest.

Peggy fell sound asleep, for she was very tired from flying in the blizzard. When she awoke the next morning, she went around the living room and noticed the presents under the tree. There was a bicycle and lovely dolls for the children of the house. Santa Claus had been there as he was every Christmas Eve.

There are very fortunate children in this house to receive these pretty gifts, thought Peggy, not knowing who Santa Claus was. Tom had told her about these houses on the way to Ocean World, and now she was in one.

It wasn't such a good idea to run away. I won't do this again. Nobody knows where I am, not even my friend Tom. He can't find me now that I am lost to everybody. Oh, what can I do? What is this place? thought Peggy, standing in the living room.

Suddenly she heard laughter and the sounds of running, and down the staircase came the two young children of the house. They both gasped in surprise when they saw Peggy, a real live penguin, in the living room.

Amy said to Chris in surprise, "What is it?"

Chris told her, "It's a penguin. They live in Alaska."

"What's it doing here?" Amy asked.

"I think it's fallen down our chimney in the storm."

"What shall we do with it?" she asked. "Is it real?"

Then Peggy quacked twice, and Chris and Amy acknowledged her message of "hello." They knew the penguin in the living room was a real penguin.

"I'm Chris. This is my sister Amy. Who are you, little penguin?" Chris asked. Amy nodded in agreement.

"I am Peggy the Penguin of Ocean World. I was flying home to Alaska, but I got lost and fell down your chimney."

"When you fell down our chimney, did you happen to see Santa Claus on the way down?" Chris asked.

"I don't know who Santa Claus is," Peggy told them.

"Santa Claus is St. Nicholas, who comes every year from the North Pole to visit the children of the world and leave them presents for the New Year. He drives his sled with very special reindeer and arrives Christmas Eve every year. After leaving his toys, he goes back to the North Pole, and he and his elves make the toys all year to leave the next year for us. Do you have Santa Claus in Alaska?"

"I think we do," answered Peggy. "He comes on a sled to Nome, Alaska, and leaves food and presents on a starry night for the children. He wears a suit of red and white, and his sled is pulled by reindeer instead of dogs."

"That certainly is Santa Claus," Chris told her. "Amy and I wait every Christmas Eve for him, and he always comes, but only when the house is quiet and we are asleep."

Then Peggy asked, "May I stay here with you and Amy? It is so cold outside and I am so tired. I ate all the cookies and drank the milk you left. I was very hungry."

"Yes, you may," Chris told Peggy. Then he turned to his sister. "Let's open our toys, Amy. I have the bicycle I asked for, and you have your new doll, Princess Faye."

"Yes, I have the doll princess I asked for. Princess Faye is so lovely, I will love her always," Amy said.

"What do you have, Peggy?" asked Chris.

"I have two new friends, and I am warm at last."

"Amy and I had a very unexpected gift this year, Peggy, and it was you. We really want you to stay here at our house and not fly away again. Will you, Peggy?" Chris asked.

"I will be glad to stay with you," Peggy answered. "You saved me from a terrible storm. Will you tell my friend Tom and my friends at Ocean World that I am here now with you?"

"Yes, and we will ask our mother if you can stay," Amy told Peggy.

Then Martha, their mother, came into the living room. When she saw Peggy she asked them, "Who is your new friend?"

Chris answered, "This is Peggy the Penguin. She was lost in a blizzard and fell down our chimney. Peggy is from Ocean World but was flying home to her family in Alaska when she got lost and fell into the living room. May we keep her?"

"Yes, you may. If Peggy wants to stay with us, we have a spare bath for her to live in. Now we will all celebrate Christmas morning with my special pancakes. Father will be excited to see your friend Peggy. Merry Christmas to you and Peggy. Let's go downstairs and eat our Christmas breakfast. Santa Claus was certainly good this year. Now we have Peggy."

Peggy the penguin stayed for many years with Chris and Amy and their family. She frolicked with their friends in the summer in the nearby lake and followed Chris and Amy on their sleds in the winter. Many a child knocked at the door and asked for Peggy. "Is Peggy home?" they would ask. "We want her to help us build an igloo like they have in Alaska. She will show us how to do this. We know she will."

Always Peggy's answer was flapping her wings and saying, "Yes, I will," and then the fun began. The children frolicked around Peggy, and together they built a beautiful igloo for all to play in. Each new winter meant a new igloo.

They celebrated each Christmas as another anniversary that they had found Peggy, cold and lonely in their living room one Christmas morning. With their parents' permission they adopted her. What a surprise for the children of their school and neighborhood. Chris and Amy had adopted a penguin. It was the talk of the family.

But soon Chris and Amy grew up. It was time to go to college. They had to leave their high school and their friends and go far away to another school in a different state.

One fine day they asked their mother and father, "As we are going away to college, may we take Peggy with us? We will miss her if she stays home."

"Your father and I have seriously talked this over, and it is best Peggy goes along with you to college so you won't be lonely without her."

"Oh Mother, oh Father, thank you so much. It's the best going-away present you could have given us," they said.

Then they both kissed their parents, and Peggy flapped her wings and quacked as only a penguin can. Peggy was appointed the college mascot upon arrival.

"I have never seen such a beautiful bird," the dean exclaimed when he saw Peggy. "With your permission, may she be our college mascot?"

"Oh yes," answered Chris and Amy. "We are sure Peggy will like this a lot." Then Peggy flapped her wings in agreement. She was to be the school mascot and graduate with them also. The school newspaper ran the story of her falling into Chris and Amy's living room during a Christmas day snowstorm and being a part of their family for many years.

The newspaper also told of her rescue by Tom, the sled dog runner in Alaska, her home, and being featured in Ocean World as a celebrity.

Peggy appeared at all the water festivals at the college. Being so popular she was often asked, "Peggy, show us the way you dive with three twists in midair."

Peggy then flapped her wings and dove head first into the pool and did three twists in the air to the amazement of the audience. The applause was heard throughout the school.

Graduation day finally arrived. The day Chris and Amy had waited so long for was at hand. When their names and their degrees were announced, another name was with them. Peggy the Penguin had earned a degree in Isometrics because of her diving skills.

Peggy approached the stadium and flapped her wings. With a "quack, quack," she accepted the honor.

A great shout of applause echoed over the lawn of the school. Peggy was an honorary member of the college now. Chris and Amy's mother and father were there and proud of their family of three. They applauded enthusiastically.

Peggy the Penguin, although lost in a cavern in Alaska, had been found by loving hands and rescued. She lived happily with Chris and Amy's family for many years and built new ice igloos with the children of the neighborhood, who came year after year.

Learn the lesson Peggy learned: Never leave home unless your parents know where you are going so they may find you again.

Merry Christmas and many more to all of you dear children. Until Santa meets you again next year, may God bless you and keep you all.

Jamie and the Christmas Wolf

Jamie's mother, Margaret, had her usual afternoon nap on the back-yard patio of their ranch house after a hectic morning of cooking and cleaning. Jamie, a mischievous, active four-year-old boy, was always told not to leave the yard until Mommy woke up.

"Jamie, do not leave the yard while Mommy sleeps" she told him. "Don't forget now."

"Yes, Mommy, I promise I won't leave the yard," Jamie told her.

But this day he didn't remember his promise, and with the endless curiosity of a four-year-old, he ventured out to investigate what was on the other side of the yard. Although the yard had a fence, there was actually a woods on the other side that was surrounded by bushes. Jamie was on his way to a new adventure, or at least that's what he thought. So he slipped under an opening in the yard fence and was off to see what was on the other side.

Much to his surprise, he saw what he thought was a small puppy by the side of the road. But it wasn't a puppy at all. It was a wolf cub. Jamie had never seen a wolf cub before.

Oh boy, a puppy for me to play with. Now I'm going to have a lot of fun, Jamie thought.

He did not realize that looking after the puppy was a large gray animal Jamie took to be a dog. But it was Tina, the alpha gray wolf, a legend in the area and leader of the pack.

As Jamie played with the cub and Tina looked on, he saw a squirrel cross his path and decided to follow it. The cub followed Jamie, and the wolf mother followed them both. Jamie was well into the dark woods with its tall trees when he realized he didn't know how to get home. It was getting dark and he was getting hungry. Then night began to fall, and the silence of the woods frightened him. By this time he was really tired and he started to cry.

"Daddy, come find me. Where are you?" he cried, but his daddy did not come. Jamie was lost. "I'm hungry. I want something to eat. Mommy, where are you?" he asked in vain. Still no Mommy and no dinner.

There was no answer from the silent forest. Jamie knew then he was lost. There was no Mommy or Daddy now. He was a sleepy little boy, and with small tears falling down his cheeks, he lay down for an exhausted nap on a grassy knoll. The wolf cub had followed his mother, Tina, to their cave. Jamie was alone in the forbidding woods and very frightened.

Suddenly in his sleep he felt a warm moisture on his cheeks. When he opened his eyes to the light of a full moon, he saw there was a huge gray dog looking down on him. But this was not a dog. It was Tina. She was a legend in the area, and many a traveler heard her mournful wail to the ancestors of her birth. They then knew they had ventured too far and to turn back.

This was the legendary animal that gently woke Jamie with her soft, moist tongue.

"Whose doggie are you? I never saw you before," Jamie said.

Tina only softly barked and gently pushed Jamie, who rose and followed her. Now that he was fully awake, he spoke to this strange gray dog. "Doggie, are you really a wolf? I want to go home." The wolf answered by licking his tears away.

The winds were getting gustier. Jamie was getting colder. He followed Tina, who led him to her cave away from the winds of fall and to safety, where to his delight there were three small pups. They were Tina's wolf cubs. He squealed and like all small boys played with them. While Jamie and the cubs were tumbling with each other, Tina brought back some wild blueberry stalks, which hungry Jamie devoured. But like all runaway boys, he really wished he was home for dinner with his mother.

Jamie then fell asleep, and when the dawn broke, he found himself warm and dry with Tina nestled beside him. But it wasn't long before the cubs woke up and disturbed his sleep. They were hungry and soon Jamie was dislodged and the cubs were hungrily feasting on their mother's milk.

But then another voice was heard. It was Daddy's voice.

"Jamie, Jamie, it's Daddy. Where are you? Jamie, son, where are you?" his father frantically called.

Jamie ran to the front of the cave, and there were his father and his uncle Ben calling for him on the bottom of the slope. Although he was happy with Tina and her cubs, he really wanted to go home. The people of the neighborhood were there, all looking for lost Jamie.

"Daddy, Daddy, I'm here. Here I am. Come get me," he announced, and his father and uncle immediately ran up the slope to the cave when they heard him call. The townspeople followed them as fast as they could.

Tina watched on silently, surrounded by her young cubs. She had no fear of man, as she had bonded long ago with him.

Jamie's father and uncle ran up to the cave and gently picked Jamie up in their arms. Silently Tina turned and, with her cubs following her, went back into her cave. Her task was done. This lost boy, Jamie, was found. The townspeople happily surrounded him, grateful he was safe. Then his father and uncle took him back to his house.

Jamie was home again, thanks to the motherly act of a wolf that had found and sheltered him. Although he loved the cubs and played with them for hours, he missed his mother and wanted to go home. He was really very hungry.

It was also known that Jamie had learned his lesson and would never stray again. The families all celebrated Jamie's return and listened to his stories of the friendly gray wolf and her playful cubs. They knew this was the legendary gray wolf, Tina. It could be no other.

Christmas morning arrived. A very happy Jamie went down to

the living room to see the tree and the presents he knew Santa Claus would leave. The tree was glowing with lights, but to Jamie's delight and happiness, in a small box was a tiny creature with a red ribbon on it. It was the puppy he had asked for. Santa Claus had brought it as Jamie had asked and he knew he would.

"Jamie, I love you," said the Christmas card greeting, and this small golden puppy did love Jamie with all his heart. And Jamie also loved this small, affectionate creature.

Jamie grew up with the golden puppy, never forgetting Tina, the grey wolf, and her puppies. It was a very strong lesson about not running away, no matter how tempting it was to explore.

That Christmas the families in the area visited their lost little boy, now found thanks to Tina. Many gifts and greetings were exchanged in Jamie's house that Christmas. Many treats were left by the townspeople in Tina's woods in appreciation of her saving Jamie. Tina and her cubs were well taken care of. She and the townspeople lived with each other in peace for many years.

Jamie grew up with his dog, now named Tina after his friend, the grey wolf who befriended him when he was lost and alone in the woods. When he became a tall teenager he never forgot Tina's friendship. Now he knew it was Tina who was his guardian angel.

Merry Christmas to all. Remember, the lost can be found as Jamie was found by Tina and miraculously returned home. Everybody has a guardian angel. Stay safe. Don't stray so we can always find you.

Tania the Snowbird

In a shallow cavern near the Bering Strait, in a raging blizzard, Tania the Snowbird was born. She was one of three snowbirds born to a loving mother who fed her young with morsels of fish caught from the nearby icy waters of north Alaska.

Tania was the first of the hatchlings to be born. She was a snow white bird the size of a bluebird and the color of the white tundra. But Tania was an exceptional bird. Her eyes were the color of the blue sky above the white snows of her home in the far arctic. She was the first of the hatchlings to fly and introduce herself into her new world of white expanse.

The first sight she saw were the beautiful lights of the aurora borealis, a spectacular sight in the frozen north country with a beautiful array of rainbow colors. Her lovely wings rose at her sides, and she took to the skies to see the new world she was in. She flew high and swift into the beautiful blue skies. Tania had eyes of blue to match her home in the tundra.

Tania was born to be swift. One morning she flapped her lovely wings and left the shelter of the cavern and her mother. She flew over the icebergs of the arctic she called home. But where was lovely Tania heading? Suddenly she saw below her some specks and flew down to investigate. There she found a new sight. A row of houses, people, and sled dogs all waiting to greet her. Yes, she had flown to Nome, the far north city of Alaska, home to what would be Tania's new family. She began following the sled dogs and the drivers, who came to know this little white bird who had appeared amongst them.

The drivers got to know her and many times saw her flying ahead of them when they delivered food and supplies to this isolated city in the far north. Tania foretold blizzards with her exciting chirping and the flapping of her strong wings. Many a driver found himself safe with her help. They knew Tania and trusted her instincts.

One such journey was so perilous that when a driver and his dogs saw the exciting chirping and Tania's wings flapping, he turned around and went back to the coastal city he had come from. Unknown to him, there was going to be a huge avalanche, and Tania had forewarned him. Her instincts of the north had not failed her and had warned her of the coming disaster. Jim Bowers, the sled driver, and his dogs' lives were saved, thanks to the quick thinking of little Tania.

Tania enjoyed her flights. It was her nature to fly above the white snows of the tundra. One such flight was when she saw the brilliant lights of the aurora borealis, like a beacon of light calling her.

What a beautiful sight, the little white snowbird thought. The lights were so cool and bright from the golden moon high above them, and Tania was drawn to them. "I wonder what is over the other side of those beautiful lights," she asked herself.

So off Tania, our little adventurous snowbird, flew, right into the lights. Then she found herself surrounded by a beautiful array of the lights of the aurora borealis. She loved it and basked in its brilliance. But what was this? There was another land on the other side of the lights! Yes, Tania had flown over the lights of the aurora borealis to a new land, but where was she?

It is very quiet over here, Tania thought. *I don't know where I am. Where should I go now?*

Two small, dwarf-like creatures were walking on the green lane of this new and unfamiliar land. They walked right up to Tania and surprised her.

"I am Sam," one of the elves said politely to her.

"I am Sammy." The other elf also spoke politely.

"Who are you, little bird? Why did you come to the North Pole?" they asked.

"I am Tania, the snowbird of Alaska. I came here to see what was on the other side of your beautiful lights. I didn't know this was the North Pole. I don't know what to do or where to go," she told them.

Sam and Sammy gave her directions. "Fly to the top of the hill and you will see a house made of gingerbread there."

Tania asked, "What is gingerbread?"

"It is the cookies we leave the children on Christmas Eve to eat Christmas morning when they open up the presents Santa Claus leaves for them every year."

"Who is Santa Claus?" Tania asked.

They both answered Tania, for Sam and Sammy were twin elves. "Santa Claus is the Christmas spirit of giving and goodwill for all on Christmas morning who believe in him and some who don't know about him yet.

"Santa Claus and his reindeer go out on Christmas Eve on Santa's sleigh to visit all the children of the world with presents and gingerbread cookies, which are a special treat to eat on Christmas morning while they open up their toys. We'll see you at the top of the hill," they told her.

"Thank you for telling me this. I must tell my friends back at home about this house of gingerbread. Where do all the toys come from that Santa Claus gives out?" asked Tania.

"We are from a family of elves. We work all year to make the toys that Santa Claus gives out Christmas Eve. We work all year for this special day, and Santa Claus has special reindeer that carry his sleigh full of toys."

"I didn't know Santa Claus had special reindeer to lead his sleigh on Christmas Eve. Who are they?" she asked the elves.

"Santa has a very special family of reindeer who carry his sleigh, but he has a very special one called Fanny. She is pure white with beautiful blue eyes that show Santa the way on Christmas Eve."

Tania asked, "Where is Fanny? I would like to see her."

The elves replied, "She's in Santa Claus's gingerbread house with the other reindeer, waiting to go with Santa to visit the children of the world with our toys this Christmas. The time to go is almost here." Then they gave Tania directions. "Fly over the green lane to the top of the hill, and Santa Claus will meet you there. Hurry before it gets dark."

At that they both resumed their walk and bid Tania good-bye. "We'll see you there," they assured her. "Good-bye for now," and they walked on.

Tania then flew over the green lane, and there in front of her was the most delightful house of gingerbread and numerous elves all working busily, building the toys Santa would bring on Christmas Eve to the children of the world. The reindeer were already hitched to the red and green sleigh, ready to go on their Christmas Eve journey. Fanny was at the front of the sleigh, waiting to start Santa's long-awaited visit to the children this Christmas.

But where was Santa Claus? Never fear, he came right out of the gingerbread house and greeted Tania.

When he saw her, he asked, "Little snowbird, do you want to ride my sleigh this Christmas and visit the children while I give them their toys and gingerbread cookies? My reindeer are ready for the journey this year. Fanny, my white reindeer, will lead us under the starry skies to the houses of the children now asleep and waiting for us. Her blue eyes are already sparkling and ready to lead us."

"Oh, please may I ride with you this year? I will have so much to tell my friends back home. I can hardly wait. May I ride in the front on your sleigh? I want so much to ride with Fanny, your white reindeer," Tania asked.

"Of course you can. Sit on the sleigh now, and off we will go under the stars to the houses of the children now sleeping and waiting for their toys Christmas morning. Hurry up and I will introduce you to Fanny. Perch on my finger and we will go out back, where my team is already hitched and Fanny is waiting for us."

Tania perched on Santa's finger.

"My reindeer are waiting. Sit on the front of my reindeer sleigh. Fanny, my blue-eyed reindeer, will carry you on her nose all the way," Santa told Tania lovingly in her ear.

Tania did just that, and perching on top of Fanny's nose, she waved good-bye to Mrs. Claus and Sam and Sammy. The elves stood, all waving good-bye also.

What an exciting night Tania had! No other snowbird ever had a night like it. She traveled on top of Fanny's nose from house to house, with stars brightly shining above them. They arrived at the houses to give out the children's toys and gingerbread cookies.

With the dawn silently breaking to herald the day and the toys given out, it was just about time to go back to the North Pole. The sleigh was empty and the toys had been given to the children with their gingerbread treat for Christmas morning.

Tired but happy, they made their way back home to the North Pole. The dawn was actually breaking at the North Pole and their gingerbread home was waiting for them. There on the ground waiting for their return was the lovely Mrs. Claus in her red and green dress with white apron, welcoming the travelers home. Santa Claus's family of elves were also happily waving to them. There were Sam and Sammy, the two twin elves, waiting for their return.

Tania waved back. "I am so glad to be back at the North Pole" she said as Santa Claus and his sleigh and reindeer landed. Tania was still sitting on the front of the sleigh with the reindeer who had given her the most exciting ride of her life. Fanny lovingly kissed Tania, who went back on Santa's finger to return to his gingerbread house.

"I must say good-bye now, but I will be back next year to give out the presents with Santa again," Tania said. "My friends at home in Alaska will worry about me, and I can't wait to tell them of my adventures over the aurora borealis lights at Santa's North Pole."

Tania's new friends sadly bid her good-bye, but they were happy when she said she would come back next Christmas to visit them again.

At that Tania waved a sad good-bye to Santa Claus and her new friends. She flew back over the beautiful lights of the aurora borealis to her home in Alaska.

The people at home were waiting, as they had seen her on Santa's sleigh with his reindeer. Their Tania was home! Oh, happy day, she was back!

"Tania, Tania!" They all circled her on the central square of the city. "Where have you been? We saw you on a sleigh, sitting on the nose of a beautiful white reindeer who actually had blue eyes! Who was that and where did you go?"

"I was with Santa Claus, giving out the toys and gingerbread to the children as he always has each year."

"Who was that white reindeer?" they all wanted to know.

"It was Fanny, Santa's beautiful white reindeer with blue eyes that showed us the way Christmas Eve. I rode on her nose all the way," she told them. "When I flew over the beautiful lights of the aurora borealis, I found myself in Santa Claus land at the North Pole."

"Then what happened?" they excitedly asked.

"I met Sam and Sammy, the twin elves. They told me to fly over the green road to the North Pole, and there I met Santa Claus and Mrs. Claus. Their family of elves make all the toys Santa and his reindeer give out for Christmas with gingerbread cookies for a treat for the children," she told the townspeople. "I had the most exciting ride of my life with Santa's wonderful reindeer. I actually rode at the front with the reindeer leading Santa's sleigh. The ride was great! I must tell you about it. It was so beautiful riding on Santa's sleigh under the stars and with Santa's beautiful white Fanny..."

"Who are Santa's reindeer?" the townspeople asked.

"They are very special reindeer who lead Santa's sleigh on Christmas Eve to travel to the children and give them their toys and gingerbread cookies," Tania told them. "They lead the way every

Christmas Eve, and the beautiful white reindeer Fanny has blue eyes that can see through the starry, moonlit night. That is the night Santa Claus gives the toys his elves make all year to the children of the world to open on Christmas day with their gingerbread cookie treat."

"Will he be back next year, Tania?" they asked.

"Yes, he comes every year. We will be the first stop on his trip, I am sure," she said. "I have to go back to my cavern now. I want to see my mother, sisters, and brothers who are waiting for me."

Then Tania flew back to the cavern to see her mother.

"Dear daughter Tania, where have you been?"

Tania told her excitedly about her visit over the lights of the aurora borealis, where she met the twin elves, Sam and Sammy, who directed her over the green road to Santa Claus's house in the North Pole.

She told her about Santa's elves, who work all year in the gingerbread house, making the toys for the children that Santa gives them on Christmas Eve. Tania's brother and sisters listened in awe.

"I had an exciting ride through the starry skies with Santa Claus and his reindeer. Fanny, the white reindeer, led the others over the skies to the houses of the children. I rode up front on Fanny's nose all the way. It was so exciting," she told her mother and her sisters and brothers. They were all very excited about Tania's Christmas Eve adventure.

"Then we left the toys that Santa's elves had made that year for the children in all the houses for their Christmas presents and gingerbread cookies for them Christmas morning," Tania said.

"Then we must all go up there next year to see Mr. and Mrs. Claus and the elves who make toys all year for the children for Christmas," her mother told her.

"Yes, Mother, I am sure they will be glad to see us next year."

"You must be tired, daughter dear. Do you want something to eat?"

Tania enjoyed the meal of fresh fish her mother had given her, and then she fell sound asleep in the cavern of her birth to dream of another trip next year to the North Pole to see her new friends, Mr. and Mrs. Claus and the twins, Sam and Sammy. She knew the elves would be waiting for her. She also knew Fanny would be waiting for her, and again she would lead Santa's sleigh and Tania would lead the sleigh with her.

This is the lovely story of a beautiful snowbird's trip over the aurora borealis to the other side of the lights and her adventures at the North Pole and Santa Claus land. Meet her new friends, Sam and Sammy, and the elves who make the Christmas toys. The wonderful trip her friend Santa Claus and Fanny, his white reindeer, made for her Christmas night is a must to delight the children. This Christmas story will delight all of you.

Merry Christmas to you and the children, and a happy New Year to all. Stay safe and well. See you all next year.

Cynthia and the Magic Apple

Chapter One: A Christmas Story

Cynthia Adams lived in Brooklyn, New York, at the turn of the century. It was a lovely, thriving seaport of incoming and outgoing cargo ships. Brooklyn at the time was noted for its export of golden delicious apples worldwide; they were sweet and delicious and as big as a man's fist. They were often called Brooklyn's delicious apples.

Cynthia lived with her parents, Margaret and William Adams, and her five-year-old brother, Danny Adams. Danny was a mischievous youngster known to climb the apple trees in the orchard for the largest of the yellow delicious apples for Cynthia and him to eat at bedtime with milk.

Margaret and William were farmers by trade. Their orchard was a mile long and just as deep with the lovely golden apples they harvested every autumn and shipped worldwide. Margaret Adams was noted for her preserves and delicious baked items that she sold at the summer fairs. Farmer Bill, as he was called, gave many a picnic with his friends with the wild pigs and turkeys he shot in the winter months. Life was good at the Adams farm.

Cynthia grew up in a large farmhouse surrounded by a field of corn and a chicken coop full of hens and young chicks. Cynthia and Danny were constant companions. They played in the fields of flowers during the summers with their dog, Buddy, who chased the birds and squirrels while they enjoyed lunch at the nearby stream. The stream was surrounded by strawberry bushes that they picked for their mother's pies and jams.

Danny was a chipper and mischievous growing boy of five eagerly waiting to go to school with Cynthia to learn to read. As small as he was, he was a big help to his father, raking leaves and shoveling snow with Cynthia. He also helped to pick the corn and luscious apples from the fields of the farm with Cynthia and his father in the autumn months.

Mother Margaret used the apples for her famous jars of applesauce and her pies. They were known countywide. Cynthia and her mother milked the ewes on the farm. Life was good, and nature was generous to the Adams. Cynthia and Danny were happy children growing up in the early years of the century in Brooklyn, New York.

Danny was very anxious to go to school. He often asked Cynthia, "When can I go to school with you? Can I go in September?" Danny knew the month because the leaves of their apple orchard turned brown.

"I will take you to school soon. You are five and old enough to go with me now," Cynthia told him. "There Aunt Fanny will teach you to read and to write and to do your numbers with the other children."

The schoolhouse Cynthia walked to during the spring and autumn was a one-room house with a wood-burning fireplace. Aunt Fanny was a spinster who taught in the one-room schoolhouse. As she had never married, she lived with her brother and sister-in-law at a nearby farm, commuting by horse and buggy. The children loved her. Aunt Fanny was strict but fair, many times sharing her lunch with an orphan who was boarded at the farmhouse of an affluent family.

In the winter the children were picked up by Cynthia's father on the way to the school. Snug and warm under blankets, they were taken to school in the harvest wagon. Many an apple was shared to the delight of the children. They laughed and talked on the way, munching the special treat left by Farmer Bill. When the blizzards came, the children stayed home.

The school was heated by a wood-burning fireplace. The parents supplied the logs from the adjoining forests. In very serious storms the school was closed. The bells of the countryside rang out the message of the school closing. No one ventured out in such weather.

The best students sat up front with Aunt Fanny, and the poorest had places in the back of the room. There was always the chance that with better grades they could move nearer the fireplace.

Lunch was a special hour watched over carefully by Fanny. The children brought their own lunches, which they shared and traded with each other. A whole hour was spent playing in the yard. Games like tag and hide and go seek were the favorites. It was a happy hour of laughter and glee. Such were the days of Cynthia and her young brother, going to the school with Fanny, the schoolteacher.

After kissing good-bye to their mother every school morning, Cynthia and Danny walked through the spring meadows of wild flowers and daisies. Rabbits and chipmunks ran across their path. The birds carried the lovely song of spring. In the autumn the trees turned golden and maroon and heralded the coming of the special holiday of Christmas. Cynthia and Danny had a happy childhood in the early years of the century in Brooklyn, New York.

Chapter Two: A Visit From St. Nicholas

In the snug house in the evening before going to sleep in her room, with a fireplace burning brightly, Cynthia oftentimes read before going to sleep. She had a delicious golden apple and a warm glass of milk that her mother gave her. Cynthia spent many happy hours before falling asleep. Danny, her brother, sat by her chair, listening to the stories, alive with interest.

This particular night was close to Christmas, and Danny was listening attentively to a story about Santa Claus called "A Visit From St. Nicholas." It was a Christmas present for the holiday season from her parents, Margaret and William. Danny was engrossed in the story while eating his own delicious apple. He was never far from his sister.

"Is it really true, Cynthia? Does St. Nicholas have all those reindeer? Do they really take him to the houses of the children with presents?"

"It says so here in 'A Visit From St. Nicholas,'" Cynthia answered him.

"When can I see him, Cynthia?" he asked.

"He comes only when you are sleeping so you can be surprised Christmas morning when you wake up. St. Nicholas comes down the chimney every Christmas Eve and leaves presents for the children," Cynthia told Danny, who was getting by now very sleepy.

"Please, Cynthia, read me more about him," he asked his sister. Then sleepy little Danny closed his eyes and fell sound asleep. The apple he was eating dropped from his little hands. His mother picked him up and put him snug and warm into her own bed by the burning brightly fireplace. In his dream, there was St. Nicholas coming down the chimney with a bag full of toys. Danny slept on, dreaming about this happy Christmas morning.

Margaret and William had a hot cup of tea before retiring. They kissed both their children good night and went to bed. The house was snug and warm, waiting for "a visit from St. Nicholas." Cynthia finished reading the book and before retiring drank her warm milk. But Cynthia's apple this evening strangely affected her. She fell into a very deep and sound sleep and dreamed as she had never dreamed before.

Chapter Three: Cynthia Goes to Nowhere

Cynthia woke up after an unusually deep sleep to find herself in an unfamiliar place. She had never seen the road before. It actually was green.

"Where am I?" she wondered. "What is this place? How did I get here? Whatever has happened to me?"

Actually, she was nowhere on earth. She was in the land of Nowhere, a land of fantasy. Then suddenly she heard a voice.

"Hello, Cynthia. How are you today?"

She turned and much to her surprise saw a large caterpillar on the road wearing a green suit and red shoes with bells.

I must be dreaming, she thought. *Caterpillars don't talk.Where on earth am I?*

"Welcome to Nowhere, Cynthia. How are you?"

"I am well. Where am I?" she asked.

"You have entered the domain of Nowhere, which is the way to the land of Somewhere. I am Charlie the Caterpillar. I am in charge of the roads here. My queen and I welcome you. She is in the pink palace just over the hill."

"Where is the pink palace, Charlie?"

"It is over the hill to Somewhere. I'll show you how to get there!"

"How do I get there, Charlie?"

"You have to go over the next hill. Then you will find it. I have to go home now, Cynthia. It is late and my wife and children are waiting for me with dinner."

"I didn't know caterpillars had families," she told Charlie.

"We do here in Nowhere."

"I want to go to my home in Brooklyn. I miss my family. It will soon be Christmas, and Danny, my brother, and my parents are waiting for me." Then Cynthia began to cry.

Charlie again told her, "Go over the next hill to Somewhere. You will find the good queen in the pink palace there. Our queen will help you go home. I'm late. I have to hurry home. See you soon." He left her and slowly crawled away.

Although puzzled, Cynthia did what Charlie told her. She had no one else to help her. She proceeded on the road to Somewhere. She saw numbered squares and decided to play hopscotch on the way.

I have to go to the other side of the hill, she thought to herself. *I have to see the queen in the pink palace. She will help me go home. I will start now,* and off she happily hopped.

Chapter Four: The Daisy Sisters

Playing hopscotch as she went, Cynthia skipped on the numbered squares of the green road.

I like hopscotch. This is fun, she thought. And so on little Cynthia hopped, hoping to get to the other side of the road to Somewhere and the pink palace of the queen. Then suddenly to her amazement and surprise she saw three blue daisies laughing and gossiping amongst themselves. Cynthia couldn't help but be amazed.

"I didn't know daisies could talk," she said to them. "Daisies in Brooklyn, where I live, are white and beautiful, but they don't talk at all."

The daisies were surprised but friendly. "We are in Nowhere and we can talk to anybody. Blue is the color of our sky. My name is Betty," said the first daisy.

"My name is Betsy," said the second daisy.

"My name is Beenie," said the third daisy. And all three daisies opened up their petals and smiled at Cynthia.

"Who are you, little girl? Where is Brooklyn?" Betty asked.

"I am Cynthia Adams from Brooklyn, New York. It is an American colony. I live with my parents and little brother, Danny," she told them.

"What do you do in Brooklyn?" Betty asked.

"My parents grow delicious golden apples to eat. We ship them everywhere. I want to go home to Brooklyn. I miss my family."

"Will you give us one of those apples?"

"Yes, if I had one I would."

Miraculously at Cynthia's feet three delicious apples appeared and rolled over to each daisy sister. As they munched happily Betty spoke to Cynthia.

"The pink palace where you will find the queen is over the hill. The queen will help you go home. Hurry so you will be there before dark. We have to take our nap now." Then all three daisy heads went down and soon they all fell asleep.

Cynthia skipped on and when she saw a giant mushroom decided to rest. She was tired too. She sat down by the side of the road, but to her surprise the giant mushroom also talked.

"Ouch, that hurts. You are sitting on my posterior," the mushroom said to Cynthia. "You sat down too hard. Please move."

Oh my gosh, even mushrooms talk here, she thought. *Where is Nowhere? How did I get here?*

The mushroom answered, "It was your wish to come here. You wished it in your dream. You wanted to make a special holiday trip. Welcome to Nowhere. Who are you? What is your name, little girl?"

"My name is Cynthia Adams and I live in Brooklyn with my parents and Danny, my brother. We grow delicious yellow apples."

"Sorry, I don't eat fruit. Bad for my indigestion."

"I understand," Cynthia said to him. "I am trying to go home in time for Christmas. I really want to be home by Christmas."

"Somewhere is over the hill to the pink palace of the good queen. She will help you. Please remove yourself from my posterior. You are hurting my stem."

"I am so sorry I hurt your posterior. I will go now," she told the mushroom. *He is grouchy but I did hurt his stem*, she thought.

Cynthia then walked on, playing hopscotch as she went.

Will I ever get to the other side of the hill? she thought. *We'll see*, and she skipped on. But she did, and what a new surprise Cynthia got.

Chapter Five: Cynthia and the Fairies of Nowhere

Finally Cynthia hopped and skipped and got to the other side of the hill. But she was nowhere in sight of the pink palace of the queen. Instead she saw the most beautiful sight she ever had seen. There were three fairies in green suits of luminous material and carrying wands of sprinkle stars. Their shoes were pointed and sprinkle stars were seen at every movement.

They floated effortlessly through the air like weightless visions. They were surrounded by myriads of multicolored butterflies. Luminous globes were floating in the air over a clear, white water lake, and at the bottom of the lake were flowers of many colors. Orange and blue fish were swimming and humming merry tunes. The lake was alive with life.

Cynthia gasped. She had never seen a sight like it before. It was so beautiful she could not believe her eyes.

The three fairies saw Cynthia and immediately surrounded her. Cynthia gasped at their luminous beauty.

"My name is Fairy Faye of the land of Nowhere. My sisters are Faith and Fanny. Who are you, little girl?" Faye the fairy asked.

"I am Cynthia of Brooklyn, New York. I am here on a wish, and I am trying to go home. Can you help me? It is Christmastime there and I'd like to see my family. I miss especially my little brother, Danny," she said.

"Your wish will be granted," Faye told her. "Go to the top of the next hill and you will see a wonderful scene."

Then the three fairies waved their wands and floated away. Cynthia found herself on the way to the pink palace of the queen of Somewhere. But Cynthia was still in Nowhere. Somewhere was nowhere in sight.

The next hill was not too far and Cynthia decided to take a nap. She fell asleep under a green tree, and when she woke up, she heard a voice speaking to her. It was the voice of the tree, a masculine voice that asked her, "Who are you, little girl? Why are you sleeping under my branches?"

"My name is Cynthia and I am on my way to see the queen in her pink palace. My friend Charlie the Caterpillar told me she would help me get home to Brooklyn in time for Christmas. I miss my family and my brother, Danny."

Cynthia then fell sound asleep again, as she was very tired from playing hopscotch on the way to the pink palace. When she woke up she thanked the tree for sheltering her when she slept.

The tree told her, "You must go to Somewhere, which is where the pink palace of the queen is. It is just over the hill."

"I will go now, my friend the talking tree. Thank you for your help."

"Be off with you before it gets dark," the tree replied. Cynthia obeyed. And off she went.

Then Cynthia continued her quest for the pink palace of the queen. But when she went to the top of the next hill, to her surprise there was an orchestra of playing cards. The four suits were actually playing music of a lovely and melodious sound she had never heard before. Hearts, diamond, clubs, and spades were all playing in unison.

Chapter Six: The Orchestra of Somewhere

It's true, I'm here. I'm in Somewhere! I can see the pink palace. Oh, I'm so happy. Thank goodness I can go home now. The queen will help me, Cynthia thought.

Then she saw the most beautiful and amazing sight. She heard melodious music she had never heard before; it was the orchestra of Somewhere conducted by the ace of hearts. It was the queen's orchestra and playing just for her.

I love these sounds, she thought as she looked on in amazement.

The conductor raised his baton and the music began. Such sounds she had never heard before. In unison each suit of cards played their instruments. The aces played the introduction, and the diamonds led the melody, supported by the clubs, and last the deep sounds of the spades all together and in unison.

"Who are you?" she asked of the heart playing card who was leading the orchestra.

"We are the queen's orchestra of Somewhere. I am the ace of hearts. With my baton I lead the other suits of cards."

"What are suits of cards?" Cynthia asked. "I never saw an orchestra before. We don't have this in Brooklyn where I live."

The ace answered, "I am one of four suits of playing cards. The aces and I lead the orchestra. The diamonds play the melodies, and the clubs support our music. The deep, rich sounds of the spades can be heard by the queen. We all play together and in unison. The queen can hear our music at all times in her pink palace. Would you like to rest and we will play for you? What is your name?"

"I am Cynthia of Brooklyn. That is where I live with my parents, Margaret and William Adams. We grow delicious golden apples for the world to eat. I wished to come here, but now I want to go home. I want to be home for Christmas, and I miss my little brother, Danny. Yes, I will rest and listen to your music, but soon I must be off to see the queen. She will help me go home in time for Christmas."

At that the ace of hearts waved his baton and the orchestra played for Cynthia while she rested on a soft mushroom for the afternoon. She was tired from her long journey. But finally she was almost at the pink palace of the queen of Somewhere.

When the concert was finished and she was rested, she said good-bye to her dear friends.

"I must go now. Thank you for playing for me. Good-bye but only for now. I shall return to your beautiful land someday. The next time I come I will bring my brother, Danny."

At that Cynthia made her way over the last hill, and there was the pink palace of the queen.

"Now I can go home. The queen will help me." She hopped, skipped, and jumped on the way to the queen's palace.

Chapter Seven: Cynthia Meets the Queen of the Pink Palace

Suddenly the palace was there, beautiful and tall in the sunlight.
How will I ever get over the walls? Cynthia thought.

She saw lying by the side of the road a broom. It read "Fly me." *I don't know how to fly a broom*, she thought. But she looked again and saw the broom said, "Ride me and I fly." *I hope this works,* she thought. She mounted the broom and suddenly with no effort was gliding up and up and up. What a thrill it was to see the ground far below. *It's really true,* she thought. *I am flying! What a wonder. The queen must be a very special person.*

Cynthia flew up and over the walls of the palace and found herself sitting in the palace courtyard. She waited patiently, and there out of the palace came a small elf-like person in a red suit and pointed shoes with bells. The bells tinkled and told her he was coming.

My gosh, she thought, *it is an elf!*

The elf asked her, "Why do you come to the pink palace of the queen?"

"I came to see the queen because I want her to help me go home to Brooklyn, where my family is waiting for me."

The elf then asked Cynthia, "How did you get here?"

"I came here after I ate a magic apple, but now I want to go home. It is Christmas and I miss my family and little brother, Danny. Where is the queen? May I talk to her?"

Then a melodious voice answered Cynthia. "Yes, you may. I am the queen of the pink palace. How, my child, can I help you?"

Cynthia turned and saw a lovely woman in a pink dress and pink slippers walking towards her carrying a pink wand, and in her arms was a pink cat with sparkling fur and a collar of diamonds.

Cynthia gasped. "It is the queen, it really is!" She immediately bowed.

"No need of that, Cynthia. You may rise now. The three fairies of the silver lake told me of your coming. Welcome to my palace. How can I help you?"

"Dear queen, I want to go home to Brooklyn. I miss my family. It is Christmas there, and I want to be with them. I miss my little brother, Danny."

"Dear lost child, I will look into my ball of wisdom, and it will tell me how to send you home for Christmas," the queen said. "Come into my palace."

The queen ushered Cynthia into her throne room, and there on a magic table was the ball of magic. "Be still, Cynthia. I am consulting the ball of wisdom now. It is done! The ball has shown me the way for you to go home," the queen said. "Close your eyes and say three times 'I want to go home,' but we will miss you, dear child. Then open your eyes."

Cynthia closed her eyes and said three times.

"I want to go home.

"I want to go home.

"I want to go home."

She felt she was spinning round and round and then she gasped. As the good queen had said, Cynthia opened her eyes, and to her happy surprise her mother and father were standing there with her lovable little brother, Danny. It was really Christmas morning! Oh, happy Christmas day!

Chapter Eight: Home at Last!

"You slept very well, Cynthia," her mother said.

"Yes, Cynthia, very well," said her father.

"You slept great," chorused Danny.

"Merry Christmas, Cynthia. We have a special gift for you this morning," her mother said.

"Oh, Mother, what is it?" Cynthia asked.

"It is a special caterpillar for your bed when you sleep at night. Danny stuffed him for you. He will keep you company, my dear child," her mother said.

"May I see it please?" Cynthia asked.

"Of course you may," Mother answered.

Then Cynthia got the happy surprise of her life. It actually was the giant caterpillar, Charlie of Nowhere. He had befriended her when she found herself a very frightened and lost little girl in a strange land.

"Oh, Mother, it's my friend Charlie of Nowhere!"

"Who is Charlie, Cynthia?" her mother asked, surprised.

"He is my friend Charlie, the caterpillar of Nowhere, who helped me in my dream when I first went there."

"You must tell us about your dream. Come, we will talk about it at breakfast, Cynthia."

"I have so much to tell you and Father. Danny will love it," she told them.

Then they all went downstairs, and Cynthia viewed the giant Christmas tree in the living room and gasped at the lovely gifts.

"Oh, Mother, just what I wanted! A sewing kit for a new dress, and a shirt for Danny. Thank you so much. I love you and Father so much, no words can tell. Merry Christmas," she said and kissed them both.

"I have a new football and a stand for a globe in my room with a globe of the world. Now I will know where our apples are going all over the world," Danny happily exclaimed.

Cynthia presented her mother and father both with a scarf she had knitted for the winter months when she was taken to school. Danny was also given a warm hat and mittens with a scarf for his trip to school with Cynthia.

"I can hardly wait to go to school. Cynthia, please take me soon," Danny said.

"I will take you first thing when I go back. Be sure of it, Danny," Cynthia told him.

He was delighted. "Merry Christmas, my beautiful sister. I love you and Mother and Father the most."

The rest of the morning was spent having breakfast. Mother's special treat of pancakes with the syrup of trees from nearby farmers was especially delicious.

Cynthia told her parents about her dream to Nowhere and the pink palace of the queen of Somewhere. She told them about the queen helping her to go home, her travels, the magic people of Nowhere, and the melodious music of the orchestra of cards. The lovely queen's wish that sent her home to her family and Brooklyn was especially interesting to her family. Her parents loved the story of her caterpillar friend Charlie. They certainly enjoyed hearing about her dream, and Danny did too. Cynthia could not be happier to be home with her beloved family.

The rest of Christmas day was spent receiving their friends and gossiping about the future of crops that year. No friend left without a gift. Their friends also brought gifts Christmas morning to the Adams' house: special jams and jellies, fruit cakes from the plentiful crops of the summer months, and everybody's dream, especially Danny's—delicious chocolate cake like no other cake ever made, just smothered with chocolate icing. Truly a Christmas day treat for all!

Finally after much celebrating, a very tired Cynthia and Danny kissed their parents good night.

"Merry Christmas, Mother and dear Father. This was the best Christmas ever. Danny, I love you so. I will take you to school the first thing when I go back," Cynthia said. "You will love the other children and learning what you should know to be a good farmer."

"Thank you, Cynthia. I can hardly wait to go to school with you," Danny replied. "I will play football with the other children at school. Thank you so much for my new football. Merry Christmas, Mother and Father and sister Cynthia. Now I have a globe to see where our apples are going. This is exciting. I love you all the most. I will always be a good boy to make you proud of me. I love you all." He smiled, then kissed all of them.

Finally tired and sleepy Cynthia and Danny again kissed their parents good night and fell happily and fast asleep. The fireplaces in both rooms roared their warmth. This was certainly a special "visit from St. Nicholas" for both children and a happy Christmas holiday for the Adams family.

Merry Christmas and many more from all of us to all of you. Be safe!

CPSIA information can be obtained at www.ICGtesting.com
Printed in the USA
BVOW030803131011

273544BV00001B/120/P